THE GUNSMITH

#94

THE
STAGECOACH THIEVES

The Gunsmith by J.R. Roberts

Macklin's Women
The Chinese Gunmen
The Woman Hunt
The Guns of Abilene
Three Guns for Glory
Leadtown
The Longhorn War
Quanah's Revenge
Heavyweight Gun
New Orleans Fire
One-Handed Gun
The Canadian Payroll
Draw to an Inside Death
Dead Man's Hand
Bandit Gold
Buckskins and Six-Gun
Silver War
High Noon at Lancaster
Bandido Blood
The Dodge City Gang
Sasquatch Hunt
Bullets and Ballots
The Riverboat Gang
Killer Grizzly
North of the Border
Eagle's Gap
Chinatown Hell
The Panhandle Search
Wildcat Roundup
The Ponderosa War
Trouble Rides a Fast Horse
Dynamite Justice
The Posse
Night of the Gila
The Bounty Women
Black Pearl Saloon
Gundown in Paradise
King of the Border
The El Paso Salt War
The Ten Pines Killer
Hell with a Pistol
Wyoming Cattle Kill
The Golden Horseman
The Scarlet Gun
Navaho Devil

Wild Bill's Ghost
The Miner's Showdown
Archer's Revenge
Showdown in Raton
When Legends Meet
Desert Hell
The Diamond Gun
Denver Duo
Hell on Wheels
The Legend Maker
Walking Dead Man
Crossfire Mountain
The Deadly Healer
The Trail Drive War
Geronimo's Trail
The Comstock Gold Fraud
Boom Town Killer
Texas Trackdown
The Fast Draw League
Showdown in Rio Malo
Outlaw Trail
Homesteader Guns
Five Card Death
Trail Drive to Montana
Trial by Fire
The Old Whistler Gang
Daughter of Gold
Apache Gold
Plains Murder
Deadly Memories
The Nevada Timber War
New Mexico Showdown
Barbed Wire and Bullets
Death Express
When Legends Die
Six Gun Justice
The Mustang Hunters
Texas Ransom
Vengeance Town
Winner Take All
Message from a Dead Man
Ride for Vengeance
The Takersville Shoot
Blood On the Land
Six-Gun Sideshow

Mississippi Massacre
The Arizona Triangle
Brothers of the Gun
The Stagecoach Thieves
Judgement at Firecreek
Dead Man's Jury
Hands of the Strangler
Nevada Death Trap
Wagon Train to Hell
Ride for Revenge
Dead Ringer
Trail of the Assassin
Shoot-Out at Crossfork
Buckskin's Trail
Helldorado
The Hanging Judge
The Bounty Hunter
Tombstone at Little Horn
Killer's Race
Wyoming Range War
Grand Canyon Gold
Guns Don't Argue
St. Louis Showdown
Frontier Justice
Game of Death
The Oregon Strangler
Blood Brothers
Scarlet Fury
Arizona Ambush
The Vengeance Trail
The Deadly Derringer
The Stagecoach Killers
Five Against Death
Mustang Man
The Godfather
Killer's Gold
Ghost Town
The Caliente Gold Robbery
Golden Gate Killers
The Road to Testimony
The Witness
The Great Riverboat Race
Two Guns for Justice
Outlaw Women
The Last Bounty

THE GUNSMITH

#94

THE
STAGECOACH THIEVES

J.R. ROBERTS

SPEAKING VOLUMES, LLC
NAPLES, FLORIDA
2015

THE GUNSMITH
#94 THE STAGECOACH THIEVES

Copyright © 1989 by J.R. Roberts

ISBN 978-1-61232-697-9

For more exciting
Books, eBooks, Audiobooks and more visit us at
www.speakingvolumes.us

Chapter One

Quartering down the long draw toward the river, Clint Adams heard the sharp crack of the Winchester, followed instantly by the shriek of the locomotive's whistle piercing into the tall blue sky, echoing off the surrounding rimrocks of the high mountains. Now, in reply to that single agonizing cry came a fusillade of rifle fire, crashing into a stunning silence. The Gunsmith watched the smoke rising from behind the low cutbank that separated him from the railroad track edging the Moose River.

"Somebody got it, Duke boy," he said softly to the big black gelding, which had lifted his head high, snorting, his ears forward and up as he listened. "Let's go." And he kneed the horse into a canter that brought them to the protection of the stand of timber that ran over the edge of the draw.

Quickly, but with caution, he worked the big horse around the thick screen of spruce and pine until from the lip of the draw he had a clear view which opened onto the scene by the end of the long cutbank. He had the full advantage of cover as well as his view of the stalled locomotive and passenger cars below him. Swiftly, he dismounted, and taking out his field glasses, positioned himself in even better cover, for he was lying down, yet still with the full sweep of vision he had enjoyed from the back of his horse.

It was the usual single, narrow-gauge track which meant that if the engine didn't get moving again, very likely a train from the opposite direction would crash into it.

At any rate, it was clear that the holdup men weren't dallying. Obviously they were professional and knew their business. They wore masks, they were heavily armed, they rode good horseflesh, and mostly their movements were controlled. Whoever their leader was, it was clear to Clint Adams he knew what he was doing.

He counted six of the bandit gang. Two were holding the train with rifles, while four went through the cars collecting money and whatever valuables the passengers had on their persons. Yet he realized that others could be out of view, hidden in the rocks above the track with rifles trained on the stalled engine and its cars. But he still couldn't see who was the leader.

By now the men had gone through the cars and were climbing down, their sacks filled with booty. Suddenly a whistle blew and Clint saw the rider on the stocky pinto pony. He wasn't a big man—in fact he looked slender—but he knew how to handle his horse. At his waist he wore a brace of holstered six-guns. Clint watched him lift his gloved hand and bring it across in a wide gesture which obviously meant it was time to move out. Smart. So many holdups were conducted with chatter and even bantering which only offered the passengers material for description when they later talked to the law. This man, whoever he was, kept his men disciplined, silent, and obviously had seen to it that no unnecessary moves were made. Clint would have bet there were more men hidden.

He watched now as the box was taken down from the express car and saw the leader of the gang ride up to it. Now, without slowing his horse—while it was still walking—he drew one of his six-guns, and with one bullet shot off the lock. Smoothly, he holstered the weapon, and pointed toward two men who stepped forward and opened the box and began pulling out gold bars. These were passed among the men who were now mounted, and in another few moments, the leader signaled with a motion of his arm. And without a word of the customary warning that nobody was to follow, they were gone.

Clint walked back to where his horse stood cropping the buffalo grass, and kicking now and again at the deer flies. He checked his rigging, mounted and rode down to the train where the engineer stood looking down at his fireman, who was seated on a tree stump and who had evidently been wounded.

The passengers were not taking it too badly. One elderly gentleman with a rush of side-whiskers put it that they had been "cleaned out!" And yet, no one had been molested. The women especially had been treated with courtesy; and there had been no attempts to humiliate any of the men. The bandits had spoken slowly and carefully, Clint learned, giving the impression that they were trying to disguise their voices, and sometimes in communicating amongst themselves they had even used hand signals.

Clint went slowly through the cars, while the

engineer and conductor attended to the wounded fireman. He had suffered a bullet through his upper arm; not serious, though painful. A condition to which his colorful profanity attested. No one else had been hurt. Somehow—and Clint caught this immediately—the careful behavior of the holdup men, their courtesy and lack of any kind of braggadocio or offensive language gave the feeling of a greater threat than if they had behaved in the usual manner of road agents, with a much looser attitude toward their victims, and often even unnecessary violence. Clint saw that the gang had given the appearance of being so well disciplined that they were far above coarse behavior or threats of retaliation should they be followed. He realized right off that not one of the passengers had even considered defying the procedure. Nor was there any deep resentment that he could see.

"What was their leader like?" he asked some of the passengers, but the leader hadn't entered the cars. No one had seen him up close. He had kept back from the center of things, though it was obvious that everyone had realized his firm presence.

"It was kind of spooky, for the matter of that," a drummer from Kansas City told Clint. "I've been held up a couple of times, on stagelines, and it was never like this."

"Like what?" Clint asked, pressing for some give-away, something about the bandit leader that might identify him.

"Like—well, smooth, I guess," the drummer said. "I dunno. Outside of losing my money it wasn't such a bad time. And also, the feller who took it asked me if I had anything else, like for when I got to where I was going. And when I said no, he handed me back five dollars. Can you beat that!"

Clint grinned. "Did you say thank you?" And before the startled drummer could reply he'd moved down the car. Whoever was running that gang, he decided, was a smart one.

"They behaved, well almost like gentlemen," one elderly lady said. And a young man with long hair and a long nose, holding a book declared that the whole operation had been almost like a stage play. He went on to say that, yes, he'd even enjoyed it; of course, except for the loss of his billfold.

"Might I ask whether you noticed anything special about the holdup, miss?" Clint asked a young woman who was in the last seat in the car.

He had spoken to the back of her head for she was looking out the window. And now she turned toward him, and he was suddenly gazing into a pair of deep blue eyes set wide apart in a face that he could only describe to himself as "beautiful." She could have been anywhere from twenty to thirty. Clint Adams' eyes, holding hers for the moment, were also aware of the high, proud bosom and the graceful neck, plus two delightful wisps of blond hair reaching over the collar of her dress.

Her look was one of appraisal; and the thought struck him that she could be a schoolmarm. There was indeed a certain crispness; yet also more than that to her. She was soft, too, very feminine, and yet obviously not the sort to put up with nonsense. Yes, he could imagine her in a schoolroom.

A brief silence had fallen between them, but for

Clint Adams it wasn't at all empty. Besides which, he felt that wonderful stirring in his trousers as those blue eyes regarded him quietly. Then, to his gratification, a slight flush touched her cheeks.

"Are you a police officer, sir?" Her voice was cool, suited to her question while keeping him at a proper distance.

"No, I'm not," the Gunsmith replied.

"Then why are you questioning me? I believe you're the man I saw riding that big black horse."

"I thought I might be able to help," Clint said quietly. He touched the brim of his hat with his forefinger. "My name is Clint Adams."

"I see. Well, thank you. I can only say that I'm glad the affair is over with, and I hope we don't reach Prairie Falls too late." And she turned back to the window.

"Then I'll ask the engineer to hurry it for you, miss," Clint said, delighted at her spirit; yet he'd felt the need to take her down a peg. But he drew no response.

Then, as he was working his way back to the engine, he was suddenly caught by something in the girl's attitude. What was it? Something had struck him, so lightly, so swiftly that it had almost passed unnoticed. Had he seen her before somewhere? There had seemed almost a slight hesitation when he'd told her his name. But he reached the locomotive and the engineer and fireman before reaching any answer.

The fireman's arm was under bandage and he was even getting ready to use his shovel.

The engineer was in a hurry. "We better git ourselves movin' 'fore the limited comes through.

They'll be wonderin' what the devil happened to us up at the switch house, I'll be bound."

He was a doughty Scotsman with a burr to match his craggy, bearded face and glinting eyes. He could have been sixty, yet he was nimble; boney too, all elbows and knees and worry over his schedule and the possibility of being hit by a train coming the other way along that single track.

Suddenly he said, "Name's McTavish." And he wiped his sweating forehead with the back of his forearm.

"Clint Adams."

"Did you find anything back there?" And he threw his head toward the passenger coaches behind him.

"Not a thing. Except, where's your conductor?"

"He's right here," said a brisk voice coming from the other side of the train.

Clint saw the uniformed conductor climbing up into the cab now. He had a black and blue welt on the side of his head, which Clint had noticed when he'd spoken to him earlier at the other end of the train.

"What did they get away with?" Clint asked now.

"Everything." The conductor stood on his firm bandy legs and spat a streak of tobacco juice into the coal bunker.

"By God, look where yer spittin'," said the fireman, speaking for the first time. He was a stocky young man with a short beard and big hands.

The conductor grinned. "Sorry, gentlemen. Thought I was home. I'll pay for washin' off the coal." He turned back to the Gunsmith, his face serious again. "They went right to the box. Knew where it was, I'm pretty damn sure. Though they pretended they didn't. That's how I sees it, and that's how I'll put it in my report. By God, I'll . . ."

The rest of what he wanted to say was blasted away in the shriek of the locomotive whistle.

"C'mon now, we got to make it through the switch or we'll be in a helluva worse jam than this here, by damn!" snapped McTavish as his hairy hand reached again for the whistle rope. "You want a ride, mister?"

"I'll stick with my horse."

"Good enough," the engineer said, and he gave two quick pulls to signal that the train was moving out.

Meanwhile, the conductor was already running his bandy legs back to his coaches, while the fireman was shoveling coal, the sweat glistening on his big shoulders as he swung the big scoop shovel.

Clint dropped down to the roadbed as the locomotive's wheels spun on the slick rails. They grabbed, and the train jerked, shaking the cars behind. He stood beside the track as the coaches rattled by him, looking up at the passing windows, watching the gestures of the passengers within as they recounted to each other the very latest version of what had happened.

All at once he saw the girl. For just a second or two. She was looking out the window. When he waved she looked away, but his own smile followed after her.

Clint Adams was still smiling as he walked over to where Duke was groundhitched. Wrapping the reins around his left hand, he grabbed the saddle horn, stepped into the stirrup, and swung up and into the saddle.

His smile had turned into a grin by the time he watched the train disappearing down the track. As he rode toward Prairie Falls, he told himself he had another reason for visiting the place. Maybe Cash Wilfong had offered him a better—or more interesting—job than he'd thought. After all, a man couldn't live by hard work alone, and those blue eyes and that high, firm bosom were enough to attract him to any one-horse town.

Chapter Two

"Something has got to be done about it, and I mean right now!" Cash Wilfong was almost spitting the words out of his mouth as he related the latest outrages to Clint Adams in the Wells Fargo office. "Otherwise, the company loses its shirt!"

The conversation had taken place two weeks earlier in the district office of the express company. Cassius Wilfong, superintendent of Wells Fargo had taken direct charge of the problem. Cash Wilfong was known as a man who got results, and he was no one to mess with. A large host of road agents had already discovered this. Yet, now in spite of his awesome reputation, a new gang had suddenly entered the game of stagecoach robbery, and was making off with plenty.

"But by God, I'm sure glad to find you in this part of the country, Clint. Now, you've got to help us. No! Don't interrupt!" Wilfong stopped his pacing and stood straight in front of the Gunsmith, a cigar butt between his fingers as he stabbed out his words in emphasis. "Somebody's onto our schedule. Somebody's working with them from the inside. Hell, man, they been robbing most every damn stage on the

Billings run, and they're gettin' away with it. They are getting away with it!" He stabbed the words with his cigar butt as though hammering them into the man seated across from him. He didn't wait for Clint to respond, but swept on.

"And I am here to do something about it. At last! And you—you, Clint Adams are that something!"

He paused, but just briefly, taking another turn around the small office. He was a man who seemed to be bursting out of his clothes, a torrent of movement, his hands and arms almost never stopped gesticulating.

"Don't argue it, Clint. I know just what you're going to say. You gave up being a lawman years ago. So what! You gave up mother's milk years ago, too. But by God you still drink—maybe not milk, but you imbibe, by God!"

"I'm not saying anything, Cash," the Gunsmith said, squeezing the words in before the next torrent fell from the big man who was glaring at him.

"What I'm really concerned about—and don't breathe a word of this, I haven't said it to anyone in the company, at least not yet . . ."

"That they'll start hitting the rail shipments." Clint, with perfect timing, had slipped the words in while the big man was taking a breath. It was a shock to Cash Wilfong, who was so accustomed to his own monologues, though at the same time he knew his friend Clint was not a man to just sit there and listen without saying anything.

Suddenly the superintendent of Wells Fargo grinned. The grin changed his whole face, his body even relaxed. Clint saw again what he'd always liked in the man; he was still a boy.

"You read my mind, Clint. And I see you're right with the situation. All to the good, my lad!"

"I take it then they've stayed strictly with the stage routes."

Wilfong nodded. "So far! God, they're clever. Like I said, they know our shipping schedules. Even when it's changed, and mind you, I've run through some dummy shipments to test them; they're not fooled. Those sons of bitches know what, when, where we ship. Clint . . ." He sat down suddenly. "Clint, I need your help." His voice now dropped to a grave register. "We are losing our ass, Mr. Adams."

"You've got to make good the losses to your shippers."

Wilfong wagged his big head from side to side. "You just know it."

Clint Adams had been hearing about the robberies. Who hadn't? They were on the swift increase in the wildest and the richest of the gold field boom towns. Week after week Billings' mines shipped their wealth, and week after week the outlaws helped themselves from the stages bearing the gold to the mint at Saddle City. "What about your shotgun guards?" he'd asked. "I know you hire the best and you pay well. But they don't seem able to stop it."

Wilfong threw his big hands toward the ceiling, raising his hairy eyebrows toward heaven, showing Clint the whites of his eyeballs. "What can they do! Those buggers simply block the road and halt the coach. They're stashed behind the big rocks lining the road. At even the thought of anyone doing anything . . ." And here the superintendent had again stabbed the air with his cigar . . . "Even the thought of resistance, or argument, why those guards have been blasted right off the box by men they can't even see! I mean—what the hell!" He threw his long arms out again and rose and took another turn around the room. Clint noticed he had a tear in the armpit of his checkered shirt.

"Clint, you've got to help us. Me!"

"Cash, you know I'd help you if I could, but I gave up wearing a star years ago. As you know. I don't want to throw in with the law again."

"Look." Cash Wilfong stood squarely in front of the Gunsmith. "I'm not asking you to take up with the law. I don't want you to sign on with the company. I want you to help me. You're the only man I know can do it. Clint, I'm asking you a favor. Can't you just look into it? Mosey around; don't ask questions but find out. You know, get the lay of the land." And suddenly, like a small boy, Clint thought, a grin swept his face. "Course I know you'll handle the lay of the land alright, my lad!" And both of them broke into laughter.

Then the moment had passed and they were serious again.

Clint's voice had been low, thoughtful as he spoke then. "All right, Cash. I'll take a look-see."

Cash Wilfong's grin showed his gratitude. Then his face grew serious once more. "Clint, you know they're going to know who you are soon as you show up in Billings. I want you to be careful."

"I'll be heading for Prairie Falls," the Gunsmith had said.

The Wells Fargo man nodded. "Good thinking. It's not far off from Billings."

"Close enough to shake hands," Clint said. "And they got mines there too. Anyway, if I hear, see, or think of anything I'll send a wire."

"Not 'if', my friend; say 'when'!" His eyes looked past the Gunsmith then. "Clint, I want you to know we're in big trouble here."

"I know," Clint had said, and his voice was grave. "But what about rail shipments; have they hit the trains at all?"

"Not yet, thank God. But Billings only got that spur a short while now."

"But you've been shipping?"

"We've made a couple of shipments in armored cars, and so far we haven't had trouble. But I expect it. Clint, I don't want you to think we'll be in the clear if we ship everything by rail."

"They will hit you."

"That is what I know."

" 'Cause I never knew an outlaw yet who wasn't ruined by success."

"This is a success I and Wells Fargo cannot afford. And neither can Bob Glendenning and his coach company. He's already lost a couple of his drivers."

"I know that. What I'm saying . . . well, you know what I'm saying."

"That we can expect it."

They were silent a moment and then Clint held out his hand. "Cash, I know and you know and everyone in this here country knows that if Wells Fargo can't guarantee its shipments then the whole country's going to be run by the road agents, the owl hooters, the gun slicks. I don't want that anymore than you do."

Cash Wilfong was grinning with relief as he shook his friend's hand. "I knew you'd come round to it, Clint. I like felt it in my bones."

"Dammit," said the Gunsmith. "I knew it too."

On that they had parted.

Now, two weeks later, riding toward Prairie Falls, he wondered whether the holdup of the train was connected with the stage robberies. The same gang? The same leader? For it had been somebody who knew his business and planned well. That was for sure. And it had been a Wells Fargo box in the express car. The holdup men had gone right to it.

But he had little to go on. He had nothing that he could wire Cash Wilfong.

The town of Prairie Falls—known more precisely as Prairie Falls and Junction—lay in a low, long valley that ran between mountains and was bisected by the Moose River. In itself Prairie Falls and Junction was no great prize; it was its proximity to Billings and its lush gold fields that had brought it onto the map. And when the railroad decided that it would be cheaper to ship gold and other items, such as passengers, general freight and livestock from this former Robbers Roost rather than from Billings, which was situated in the higher, rocky terrain, then the Junction took a new life for itself.

No question about it, this was bandit country. The famed Miller Rhodes gang had made this particular part of the country the most exotic of the various Robber Roosts. The valley was an impregnable fortress. The high rocks which ringed the rim afforded Rhodes and his men plenty of ambush points. The law swiftly discovered that to ride into Prairie Falls and Junction was the same as walking into a massacre trap. Pretty soon the law left the place alone, save, of course, for those who chose to remain there permanently.

The Rhodes gang finally went out of business when their leader disappeared. No one knew the end of Miller Rhodes. Some stories claimed he went to South America, no one was certain; there were many divergent rumors. The gang vanished. Some were later recognized elsewhere as being former members of the famed gang, and were either shot or apprehended by the law. In fact, all known members were finally accounted for one way or another; save for Miller himself. It was even rumored—and there were dozens of rumors—that he had died with his boots off, in bed, of old age. If anyone knew the truth they weren't telling.

For a while Prairie Falls and Junction languished, but presently the town had become—as well as a shipping point for ore—a resort for those who earned their daily bread not by honest toil, but with card and dice and con game. But after another while the cluster of frame houses and log cabins—plus two brick buildings recently erected—had grown also into a community of a number of solid citizens—shopkeepers, blacksmith, tailor and barber and such—always along with the gambling folk and the ladies of pleasure, as the newspaper writers back East called them. But it was the dealers and wheelers, card mechanics and dice arms and the frisky girls who carried the lure of excitement. Still, no one had ever been able to figure out how the town had gotten its name. Prairie Falls? There were no falls, and damn little prairie. And Junction? Some said it was from the railroad, when the track laying gang had camped there. But others recollected the time when the name was around—Junction—long before there ever was a railroad about the country. On the other hand, nobody really cared.

It was high noon when the Gunsmith rode in off the trail which fed right into Main Street. The town was dozey under the hot sun. There was little action along the street which had high boardwalks, paralleling the dried mud that had been churned up by horses and wagons, and people too. There were mostly men about, though Clint did catch sight of some women— two accompanied by men, one by a child who was holding her hand, and one who was limping along with a cane.

Clint didn't linger. He rode right to the livery and unsaddled Duke and gave him a brisk rubdown, watered him, checked his shoes and hocks and forked hay for him. Then he poured oats into the feed box.

"That oughtta take care of it, my friend," he said.

"That's a piece of hoss you got there, mister." The old hostler stood in the alley between the stalls with his head cocked at his new customer.

"That he is," Clint said. "And I want you to take good care of him. You won't be sorry."

"Won't be sorry if I do, but goddamn sorry ifn' I don't," the old man said, crisp, and began sucking his gums.

Clint didn't laugh at the humor, but kept a straight

face. "Where's a spot to throw my duffle?" he asked.

The old-timer threw his thumb over his shoulder. "There is the Junction House, other end of Main Street. And they is the Rimrock down next to the cabbage patch, 'cross the tracks. You'd be gettin' full treatment there, young feller. And then . . ." His eyes threw upward as he jerked this thumb toward the loft behind him. "They is the Hayloft Inn. Cost you two bits."

All this was said without a change in the vinegary, wrinkled face.

"Have you got a barber in this town?" Clint asked.

"Sure have. Clem Fiddle. Up Main Street a piece, on yer right. Happens to be my brother, so I know he is good at his trade."

"He got a bath?"

"Nope. But they got a bath up near the Pastime. Ask for Clyde. Clyde Fiddle. He'll handle it."

"Your brother?" Clint asked.

The old man nodded. "Got good hot water and soap. And you look like it wouldn't be a pain to you. No offense, young feller."

"Mr. Fiddle, have you got other brothers?"

"Sure do. There is Clinch, he takes care of the undertaking and buryin' and all like that. Then Clancy, he swamps out the Hard Dollar Saloon. Now and again works the sober side of the bar when things is busy."

He paused.

"That it?" Clint asked. "Clem, Clyde, Clinch and Clancy Fiddle?"

"And meself!"

Clint held up his hand. "Don't tell me. Let me

guess." He watched the old man's jaws working fast as a prairie dog's on his chew as he waited; then suddenly he let fly a string of yellow and brown tobacco and saliva, which came within a whisker of hitting a pack rat running bold as brass right across the corridor dividing the stalls.

"Clarence," Clint said.

"Wrong. Had a brother Clarence, but he up an' died on us." He spat again, swiftly, and this time with accuracy as he hit a tick that had fallen off one of the horses. "Reckon you've given up. Name here is Clint." Pause while he spat again; his jaws working now as he said, "Clinton's the name. Same as yourn', 'ceptin' I ain't no gunsmith." And he just stood there in front of Clint Adams, while his jaws worked even faster with the victory.

Looked at from the outside there wasn't a thing to choose between the Junction House and the Rimrock. And even though the old-timer at the livery had pointed out that the Rimrock came with "full treatment," Clint decided on the Junction House.

The stubby frame house stood at the far end of town, though not out of calling distance from the nearest saloons. Unpainted, its wood front looked like it was about to curl up and collapse. The shade offered by its wooden canopy did nothing to soften the heat that bore down on the entire community. There were two rockers on the porch, but nobody sitting in them. And yet it was cool in the front room. The musty smell hit Clint the moment he walked in, but he appreciated the change of temperature. A strange figure stood behind the desk, regarding him as he approached carrying his war bag and rifle.

"I take it you want a room, sir." The tall, imperious figure stood firmly in a black garment, which Clint supposed to be a gown. It covered the woman totally from the neck down, falling over the edge of her huge bosom as it dropped out of sight below the desk. Clint would have bet it went all the way to the floor. Fifty, he judged; and still scrutinizing him through her pince-nez, with the gold chain disappearing into an incredible nest of orange hair.

"You read my mind," the Gunsmith said pleasantly as he dropped his duffel and leaned the Winchester against the side of the desk.

"It'll be a dollar a night, mister. Payable right now."

These words had been spoken without the slightest expression appearing in the large, moonlike face, which was also very white, allowing a place for the small mouth, the shiny, marbled forehead—Clint thought of the smallpox—and very large ears. Yet it was the size of the lady that Clint found so impressive; though, now on second thought, it was the shape, or shapelessness that really drew his interest; and for a moment he even wondered if it was a woman. For the voice had been gruff, and the hands, which she now brought into sight as the register appeared and the pen for signing, were also large, with knuckles hardly defined in the wrinkled flesh. No, Clint decided, she had to be sixty.

"I don't know how long I'll be staying," the Gunsmith said.

"In this town you either stays a short time or

forever—permanent," the figure behind the desk said.

"Are you the owner, manager or something?" Clint asked.

"Both. And troubleshooter. The name is Carmela, but I ain't Mex. Irish. I can do anything a man can do—with gun, whip, rope, me fists."

"Anything?" Clint asked in astonishment.

"Except piss standin' up off the end gate of a moving wagon."

"Boy, I'm sure glad I can do something you can't," Clint said, reaching for the pen.

"Forgot to say I can outtalk anybody, any time, even them bullshitters what come off the trail lookin' for some free and easy for free. So don't be funnin' me, mister." All said without the slightest change of facial expression. It was like listening to an oracle, or someone reading a proclamation of war.

Clint Adams signed the register, then dropped money onto the desk. "For a couple of nights," he said. "Till I get the lay of the land."

"She ain't in this hotel, mister. And you can understand right now the management don't put up with no skylarking."

"Skylarking?" Clint's mouth formed an "O" in surprise at the quaint word for such activities.

"Fucking," the lady said, reading the name in the book, "Clint Adams. Well, I'll be. You be that Gunsmith feller."

"That is what some people call me," Clint said.

"What do you call you?"

"I just wrote it in the book there. Now, give me a key to my room, or give me back my two dollars."

This change of tactic on the Gunsmith's part brought a change of expression in the large moon-white face. Clint had to guess, but he thought she was smiling.

Suddenly the woman who called herself Carmela, brought her hand up over the edge of the desk, licked her forefinger and then drew a straight line in the space just in front of her, as thought making a mark on a blackboard or in a notebook. "One for you, by damn." And she dropped the room key onto the counter. "No visitors, exceptin' you pays the management five percent."

Clint had started toward the big wide stairs that led to the floor above. He stopped and turned. "I don't ever pay for my pleasure," he said. "It's a rule and a habit. So there won't be any percentage." And he turned and started up the stairs, feeling those tight eyes on his back, waiting for the malevolent comment. But to his astonishment, his hostess remained silent.

The Moosehead Saloon and Entertainment Pavilion furnished liquor, beer, and girls—even as its name implied. The whiskey was rotgut, as the Gunsmith had supposed it would be, and the girls were tired looking; also as he had supposed.

The bartender must have read his thoughts as he stood at the long mahogany surveying two of them coming down the stairs from the rooms above.

"They might look a piece weary, but they know their business," he said, cheerfully wiping the bar in front of Clint.

"How'd you know I was thinking that?" Clint asked, pushing his glass forward for a refill.

"It's what everybody thinks when they come to Junction. Same in all the saloons, not just the Moosehead. Short on women, the West is. I bet you already figured that one."

The Gunsmith sighed, leaning his elbows on the bar. "Mines pretty busy, huh?" He dropped the words conversationally onto the bar, and waited casually for a response.

The response came from an unexpected source.

"How busy are you, mister? Want to buy me a drink?"

The bartender had leaned on the bar now, as thought waiting for his customer's reply. Clint took one look at the girl, decided he'd been wrong about the quality of the Moosehead merchandise and nodded to the man behind the mahogany.

"I'm buying you a drink," he said to the girl. "But I'm not paying for anything else."

She was young, fair, with a full, wide mouth, a cute nose, and obviously firm, young breasts under her green satin gown. The nipples were prominent; as he eyed them, they seemed to grow larger.

The girl's look was one of surprise. He liked her eyebrows which arched slightly over her green eyes. "Are we talking about the same thing, sir?"

Clint grinned. He liked the "sir."

"I am. I never pay for it."

"Then why are you wasting my time?"

"Why are you wasting mine?"

They had moved over to a free table, pushing through the crowd which had become more noisy.

"Didn't figure I was," she said. "But I'm in this business to make a living."

The Gunsmith pulled out a chair for her, and waited until she sat before seating himself. He saw that she liked that.

"My mother taught me good manners, and I've never been able to break the habit."

She laughed at that, her whole face lighting up. There was something he liked about her that was more than just her good looks and fine figure. Yes, she definitely had something more.

"I'm curious," she said. "Why don't you pay for it like everybody does?"

Clint took a drink, and watched her as she followed suit. "Look, I get pleasure, and I hope you do, too. If you don't, then you shouldn't go to bed with me. See, it's shared. Both get pleasure; so why pay? I hope that I give as much as I get. That's how I see it." He took a quick drink and put down his glass and stood up. "Nice meeting you." And he started to turn away.

The girl didn't move.

His back was to her as she said, "My name's Hallie. What's yours?"

He might have known! Yes, he could have predicted it! The bedsprings were the noisiest he'd ever encountered, the bed the most rickety, and the sound of their thrusting bodies—not to mention the girl's squeals of ecstasy—were creating a racket that Clint knew would shortly draw fire.

This realization didn't stop him or even slow his surge toward the exquisite climax that was building. She was fantastic, following each move he made, each thrust, wiggle, stroke, pause, as though she was his shadow. She had a superb body, with tight, highly mobile buttocks, an absolutely free pelvis, and a tight vagina which held his penis like an eager hand. They were both soaking as their pace increased, along with the girl's moaning, the whining and screeching of the ancient bed; while their loins thrashed each other faster and faster until he could hold it no longer—nor could she as she cried out: "Come! Come! My God, come!"

It was at that very peak that the groaning, clanging bed collapsed, accompanying the tremendous explosion of their orgasms. And to be sure, Clint continued as they lay with the bed on the floor now, stroking deep and high inside her to the last squirt, while she clutched him with her arms and legs, her heels digging into his back, her fingers gripping his pumping buttocks.

It was at that precise moment—when the bed crashed—that the roar rose from below. And as they continued, curses rose, and there came a pounding on the ceiling. Finally, angry steps on the stairs and a hammering on the door. And Carmela's voice bellowing: "By God, that one's gonna cost your gun *ten* percent, Mr. Gunsmith!"

Chapter Three

Clint had already checked out Clyde Fiddle's "Hot Water And Soap Bath," prior to his meeting Hallie the blonde in the Moosehead, and subsequently bedding her at the Junction House. Now, after settling damages on the ancient bed with Carmela, he decided that he would get a haircut and shave at Clem Fiddle's Tonsorial Parlor.

Emerging into the hot street of late afternoon, he remarked to himself that he didn't yet need the services of Clinch Fiddle's undertaking parlor, and settled for the Hard Dollar where—so Clint Fiddle had informed him—brother Clancy swamped out and occasionally served the customers.

Indeed, it was Clancy Fiddle himself who eyed him from the business side of the bar, with all the friendliness of a malevolent rattlesnake.

Clancy was a knobby man, who looked to be all corners. Probably sixty some, Clint figured, with a long, inquisitive nose, big knuckles on his stubby hands, and with his lips and lower jaw in almost constant movement, as though he was trying to work some piece of food to the front of his mouth for spitting. He was almost totally bald, the wrinkles on his forehead climbing way back, almost onto the top of his head it seemed.

"Will it be whiskey then?" he inquired, pushing the rank smelling bar rag over the mahogany, quite aimlessly, but with his real attention fully on his customer. Clint wondered if brother Clint Fiddle had passed the word on him. It seemed everyone in town knew he was here, was aware of his reputation, and was very likely wondering why he happened to be in Prairie Falls and Junction.

Clint wondered too. For he knew full well that it was going to be anything but easy digging out information on the road agents who were costing Wells Fargo such tidy sums of money.

"It'll be your best whiskey, not the trade stuff."

"We sell the best only, mister."

"I'll let you know after I've tasted it," Clint said, having decided on the best approach to Mr. Fiddle, who was obviously a past master at the art of give-and-take information and gossip.

Disdaining to respond to the Gunsmith's sour remark, the bartender simply poured. Clint lifted his glass and sniffed, tasted, made a terrible face and then said, "It'll do; but I sure wouldn't want to give it to my hoss."

Clancy Fiddle, being an ace at social maneuvering, had changed his tactics completely, and now smiled, revealing a few teeth missing.

"Nice looking piece of hoss flesh, that animal of yourn," he said, his truculence having turned full circle to amiability. Clint knew Mr. Fiddle was not a man to trust out of his sight. At the same time, as with his brothers, there was something he did like about Clancy.

To Clancy's remark about Duke, Clint nodded. "Just had a bean shave from your brother across the street," he said, to keep things going.

Clancy leaned his knobby elbows on the edge of the bar. "Clem, he gets some corkers in there, by golly. Told me, a old bugger come in the other day and sat back in the barber chair, and when Clem asked him whether he wanted a shave or haircut the old geezer up an' said, 'Just cut my throat from ear to ear.' " At which Clancy slapped his palm on the bar, turned away, bent limp with silent laughter; turned back to Clint, his eyes nearly closed and sprouting tears of hilarity, slapped the bar again, gasped for air, bobbed up and down a couple of times, finally managed to recover. "How about that son of a bitch, huh? A corker, by Jesus!"

Clint had joined the laughter, though not as graphically as the storyteller, and in fact he was more amused in Clancy's rendition than in the actual story.

Clint was about to say something that would lead toward the train robbery he'd witnessed, but Clancy beat him to it, which was all to the good.

"Heard you got messed up in that train robbery at Moose River."

"Funny thing, I just happened to be riding along on my way here when I heard the whistle, and then a lot of gunfire, and I rode over for a look see."

"An' by God, there she was—huh? . . ."

But a couple of customers wanted drinks, and Clancy had to leave before anything more could be said. It gave the Gunsmith time to think out his strategy. Then Clancy was back.

"Heard they got away with a big one," he said, still pushing his rag over the top of the bar. Then he leaned forward on his forearms. "I hear nobody could identify them. That true?"

"They were all wearing masks," Clint said. "And they all had guns, what's more."

"You don't have a notion who they was?"

"I sure don't. All I can say is they did their job fast, quiet, and like they knew what they were doing."

"What d'you mean by that?" Clancy leaned closer, his eyes right on the Gunsmith.

"I mean, they didn't waste time with a lot of talk and horsing around."

"Then they just hauled ass, huh?"

Clint nodded.

"Couldn't get a look at a one of them?"

"I had no reason to. But I don't believe anybody recognized or could describe any of them."

"Too bad," the bartender said.

Clint wondered how much he meant that.

"Did you get a look at their guns, their horse-flesh?"

"I was pretty far away."

"Didn't have glasses, huh?"

Clint remembered his field glasses in one of his saddle bags that he had left at the livery. The livery brother could have easily discovered them and passed the word on to Clancy.

"Horses were in good shape," he said. "But I couldn't see close on their weapons." He kept his tone bland, innocent. But he knew very well what Clancy Fiddle was after.

"Sometimes a man can recognize hosses," Clancy said. "Them bandit fellers, they generally have good mounts."

"If they know their business, they can do a little painting," Clint said.

"I see you know the business some," Clancy said, grinning. "You're sayin' they can paint out a blaze or stockings, and even paint 'em in."

"It's been done often enough," the Gunsmith said.

Clancy Fiddle leaned forward and dropped one eyelid in a long knowing wink.

"That the first train that's been held up?" Clint asked smoothly.

" 'Pears so. The boys bin workin' the stage runs. Trains, well, that's not so easy; not that I'd know one way or th'other," Clancy concluded, innocent as a harp, and then moved away to serve a customer at the other end of the bar.

Clint nursed his whiskey. He didn't want it really, but it was after all a necessary cover for standing there chatting with Clancy Fiddle. He was pretty sure now that Clancy knew a good bit more than he was letting on. And he wondered about his brothers, whether they had connections with the road agent gang.

He saw that Clancy was staying down at the other end of the bar, and this increased his suspicion that the man knew more than he'd been telling about the holdup. He was pretty sure a number of people in Prairie Falls knew more than they were telling about the Billings and Wells Fargo holdups.

He was just putting down his glass when he felt the

man behind him. He had been standing at the bar a
few feet away during his conversation with Clancy
Fiddle, and Clint noticed every once in a while that he
had somehow edged closer. It didn't seem like anything special at first, but then, testing it, Clint had
moved away, just to see what the man would do. He
was a medium-sized man looking to be in his early
forties, with a smooth face and hands, a trim mus-
tache, but otherwise clean shaven. Clint took him for
a gambler.

It was when he had decided to leave the saloon that
he felt, more than actually saw, the man move closer
to him. Suddenly the Gunsmith turned toward the
man who was getting ready for another move closer.

"Getting too tight for you down that end of the bar,
mister?" Clint said casually, but there was an edge in
his voice that was unmistakable.

The flush of surprise at being caught out was
clearly evident in the other man's face, but he was
quick—as any gambling man—and covered with a
little laugh. "Just hoped to have a word with you, Mr.
Adams. But I didn't want to intrude, wanted to pick
the right opening."

"Thoughtful of you," said the Gunsmith drily.

"A man like you—with your reputation—has got to
be tired of intruders, I'd say. I would be, were I in
your shoes. Reckon I should've spoken right up
without all the shilly-shallying."

Clint had turned fully toward him now, facing him
squarely. "Then why don't you right now?"

"Can I buy you a drink, sir?" And he nodded
toward a table in the corner of the room.

Clint allowed a moment of hesitation to hit the

other man, and then he said, "I am figuring that what you've got to say is important."

"That it is, sir!" And smoothly, he turned and signaled Clancy for the bottle with a flick of his forefinger. Obviously he was known in the Hard Dollar, obviously he was respected; and it was obvious too, that it was a respect born of fear.

Clint Adams registered all that in a flash as he walked, not toward the table the other had indicated, but to a table beyond.

His companion was smiling as they sat down. "I see you're a man who knows his own mind, Mr. Adams."

"I can't say I know anyone else's I'd rather know," Clint replied.

"My name is DeWitt. Harry DeWitt, referred to sometimes as Ace DeWitt." And he held the bottle over Clint's glass for a second before pouring, waiting for permission as it were. "By the way, I own this place."

Clint nodded. "That'll do her."

"I'll not waste your time," DeWitt said. "I know who you are. I don't know your business here, and I don't want to. I want to make you a proposition."

"You want to hire my gun."

A smile quickly touched DeWitt's eyes and narrow mouth, but was replaced by a look of gravity. "Not exactly. Let me put it that I wish to engage your talent."

"Put it any way you like," Clint said. "My gun is not for hire."

Ace DeWitt was holding up his slim hand in protest. "I see no problem there. What I am asking you is to do some investigative work for uh, myself, and my associate, who must remain unknown. For the present," he added quickly.

"Sounds pretty fishy to me," Clint replied. Yet he felt his interest rising, for it was obvious Ace DeWitt was no small-timer. "But I'm still listening," he said.

Ace DeWitt touched the side of his chin with his forefinger, pursing his lips, as though searching the way to begin, and then said, "My associate—let's call him X—is in charge of a large enterprise that, well, could be of great benefit to everyone in the West. It has to do, briefly, with a new kind of water piping, that is to say, irrigation. You know very well how this particular part of the country is almost bone dry. X has the remedy, but it is still not quite ready for the market."

"And you're concerned about a competitor, or possible competitor who is onto his plan and wants to steal it."

DeWitt's surprise was swift. "Capital! I knew you were the man for us. In point of fact, it was I who recommended you, brought your name into X's presence!" He was smiling all over his face.

"You want to know what the competitor knows," Clint said, realizing with interest that DeWitt had overtones of the English. His choice of words such as "capital" and "in point of fact," plus a slight accent told him this. Was he fronting for an English company? One of the many that were coming into the West, though most of them were in cattle. And of course, as DeWitt had indicated, water was of prime importance in this area.

"Look, Adams, it's relatively simple, though it

requires a man of intelligence. That's to say, a man of tact, patience, and possibly courage. All of which you certainly have in bountiful amount!"

"Who is it you want information on? Mind you, mister, I am not saying I will do this. It's not my line, spying. So I'm being open with you. Maybe there's something more to it than you're telling. In fact, I damn well know there is."

Ace DeWitt had been on the point of objecting, but stopped, witholding the comment that had sprung to his tongue, and now relaxing, he sat back and regarded Clint Adams carefully.

"I'm going to have to trust you. I mean, I do trust you. Indeed, I wouldn't have approached you in the first place had I not trusted you." He paused, looked down at his drink, but didn't reach for it. "It's a situation I want you to look at, not necessarily a person. Although there may be a person or persons who come into it. That I cannot predict. But the main thing X wants to see clearly is the situation. The lay of the land . . ." And here he paused to take a drink, while Clint suddenly remembered Cash Wilfong's joke about "the lay of the land," and there had been Carmela's feisty remark when he'd checked in at the Junction House. But DeWitt was speaking again.

"What is needed is an unbiased opinion, plus facts of course, on the current as well as projected need for water in the Billings area. It is possible that there could be a larger opening towards cattle drives coming north from Texas. As you know, the herds, when they reach their northern destination remain for some time fattening on gramma grass, and certainly there is the need for water. Then too, there are farmers coming into the country; the land is dry, and that's not good for growing. But there can be irrigation, and that means the transportation of water from, say here to there." He demonstrated by touching one side of the table, then the opposite side. "Is this feasible, is it possible? You are not only a noted upholder of the law, though no longer an officer as I understand you used to be, but you are trusted by a great many people. Whereas myself, a noted gambler, would fall under immediate suspicion. What are they asking about water for? What are they planning to do? All of that. You understand? We simply need to see what is possible for a proposal that in itself is not only intelligent, but would be highly profitable and useful to cattlemen, farmers, and the land in general. It is a service, and one in which X and his associates firmly believe in. They are of course hoping to make money, but a reasonable amount for their trouble, their enterprise; and moreover they will be helping in a really good way to build the West."

"Let's get to the point," Clint said. "What exactly are you asking me to do?"

"I want you—just casually, mind you—to keep an eye on a certain person who is connected with a group that wants to break up our enterprise, sabotage it."

"This group doesn't want your water, your irrigation facility, is that it?"

"They're land grabbers, to be more precise. They're afraid that if the government backs our water plan—that is, if we can get water to certain sections of land that will assuredly benefit—then the land will be thrown open to homesteading."

"I see. But what *exactly* do you want me to do? I'm

not agreeing to go along, mind you, but I'm asking for some clear idea of what it is you really do want."

"To be precise, I want you to contact a certain woman who is connected with the Ajax-Hiller Company, the group in question. Now look . . ." He held up his hand. "I know you said you're not a spy person, but I am not asking you to follow anyone, nothing like that! I simply want to know what you can pick up about this person, as it were, by the way."

"You sound crazy to me," Clint said with an easy smile, only his eyes were not smiling. He stood up. "What do you take me for? Do I look like someone who'd fall for a cock-and-bull story like that!"

"Hold hard! Wait a minute, sir!" Ace DeWitt held up both hands, imploring the Gunsmith not to leave.

Heads turned, then returned to where they had been before. Anything could happen in a place like the Hard Dollar. Clint saw Clancy Fiddle watching them from the bar.

"Please sit down, Adams. I think you will be interested—definitely interested—when I tell you who the person is I want you to keep an eye and ear on; though I repeat—casually, easy!"

Clint remained standing, looking down at the other man. "I'm listening."

"The person is a woman named Melanie Lansing."

"Never heard of her."

"You will, whether you take me up on my offer or not."

"What do you mean by that?"

"I mean this," DeWitt said, jabbing his middle finger into the tabletop. "Lansing is a writer, and she is looking for you. She plans to write the story of your life for an eastern magazine. Your life, Adams. Mr. Gunsmith."

"I thought you said she was connected with some company."

"She is. She is also a writer."

"You want me to dig some dirt on her. That's not my line of business."

"No," said DeWitt. "I want information. Look, Adams, she's got you two ways from the jack. If you don't talk to her, she'll write anyway; she'll make it up."

"Mister, my life is my personal property."

"I know exactly how you feel. But this woman is going to spread you all over the East. She has no scruples." He took a swift drink. "See, why not speak to her, find out her angle, see if you can soften what she writes; bring her to a truer, more realistic, more appropriate life story. And meanwhile . . ." He opened his hands, a careful smile on his face, watching for Clint's reaction.

"Meanwhile—what? You're suggesting two birds with one slug? I feed her a so-called favorable story about myself, or let's say one I can hide behind, and at the same time pick up dirt for you?"

"Bravo! That is precisely what I am after. I couldn't have put it better myself! She, let us say, is bent on getting information out of you, and that can be the information you want her to have, nothing more; and meanwhile, you will be getting whatever you can from her and turning it over to me. She will be so eager to get your story, her guard will be down."

"And you think she's going to spill stuff just like that? You're crazy."

"She won't spill anything, in the way of precise information, but she may reveal something to an astute eye such as yours, or mine, say. Without realizing what she's doing. It's a wild chance, but I'm a gambler. I know that it's not impossible for the long shot to pay off. You see . . ." He tapped the tabletop with his middle finger. "Details, my friend. Details are always essential to a plan. And it is always on the overlooked detail that success and failure turn, in the casual remark or gesture." He took a pull at his glass, touched the end of his nose with his forefinger and said, "All for a substantial fee, it goes without saying."

Another pause followed, while the Gunsmith studied the man seated in front of him. DeWitt's elbows were on the table, his hands were clasped together in front of his chin.

Finally, DeWitt opened his hands, still with his elbows on the table. He leaned forward now, lowering his forearms. "Well, what do you say, Mr. Adams? Once again the name is Melanie Lansing and she is stopping at the Junction House."

Clint knew that was as far as the conversation was going to get, and still there was something that caught him, something that pulled at his interest. Clearly, DeWitt was a sharp one, and yet his proposition sounded like an amateur had dreamed it up. He stood up.

"Mister," he said slowly, taking plenty of time. "I say if you handle the cards like you dream up propositions then you sure ain't going to die happy and rich."

He watched the smile drift into DeWitt's face, and then he turned and walked out of the saloon.

Outside in the street the sun was bearing down, and just going past him was a ten-mule wagon stirring up a great cloud of dust. Suddenly he saw the woman he'd talked to on the train. She was on the boardwalk on the other side of the street gazing intently into a shop window. He could only see her profile, but he was sure it was she. And as he stood there staring at her, he all at once felt something strike through him. It was a kind of recognition, though he wasn't sure of what.

And yet he knew he had hit the right note with DeWitt. Scoffing as he had was surely the right gesture; indeed, the only gesture that a man such as DeWitt, putting his proposition in such a way, could expect.

The point was clear that the man didn't want to say in exact words what he really wanted. It was only too obvious to Clint that DeWitt was deliberately drawing a vague picture, wanting him to fill it in for himself. In that way, nothing incriminating would have been said. In that way the whole operation would be put into play by Clint Adams. DeWitt had actually said nothing. Yet he had implied a great deal. And at the same time, it was obvious that the gambler had intentionally spun a story he knew Clint Adams would not believe.

The boys in the upstairs room over Shoshone's Red Eye Saloon were enjoying a satisfying moment. The game was stud, the deck was stacked. They had just taken the half-breed Cherokee, a stranger in town, for close to two thousand dollars. The Cherokee, a nineteen year old named Tiny Blue, had come to town only that afternoon. It was rumored that he had sold his cattle, though some of those present thought he must have gotten his two thousand by less strenuous means. Now, stripped of his "hard-earned" money, he left the gambling den with an extremely forlorn expression on his young face.

"Tiny Blue, what the hell kind of monicker is that?" said one of the card sharps with a loud laugh. "He's even tinier now, without all that money to pump him up, by God."

"Bastard don't have a pot left to piss in," said another.

"What the hell," said a third. "All he'll be pissing into now will be the wind!"

The young half-breed's money lay on the tattered baize-top table in large bills. In order to divide it, the gamblers produced their own rolls and busied themselves changing their newfound riches into equal shares. But since each was highly distrustful of the rest, they were therefore so intent on the division of the spoils that they failed to notice the woman who entered the room.

Had they looked at her under any other circumstances they would surely have agreed that she was a handsome creature—glistening black eyes, long black hair, and bold, exotic features. Her figure which was obviously free of any corset, was in the admired hourglass shape. On the other hand, she wore a cowboy's wide-brimmed black hat, a man's jacket and pants, plus boots; and most important, around her slim waist a brace of cartridge belts with holsters. One holster was empty, the other filled.

As the young lady tiptoed forward now, she held a .36 caliber revolver made by the Manhattan Firearms Company. The six-gun had a pearl handle, as did its companion in the other holster. Suddenly she fired, splintering the poker table, sending a shower of cards, chips, and banknotes and coins in all directions, causing the astonished faces of the gamblers to turn white, tinged with ash gray.

" 'Scuse it, gentlemen," the lady observed coolly, "but I believe you just gave a young Indian some lessons in stud poker. He claims the lessons were just too damn expensive. Now next time you strip a Cherokee, pick one who's not my husband." Her smile was broad, her black eyes glittering. "Now then, unless you don't give a damn what's going to happen next, you'll just do as I tell you."

At that point she took off her hat and handed it to the nearest gambler, while the hard round hole of the revolver's barrel seemed to cover each of the stricken gamblers at once as they stood there frozen into the extraordinary tableau. There was no hesitation as they moved to obey the lady's commands, to pick up all the money from the floor and table, and also to empty the contents of their pockets into the hat.

At the same time, she relieved them of their weapons, hurling the guns out the window and into the back alley. Then, as quickly and silently as she had appeared, she was gone. The gamblers, now considerably poorer, waited a few moments, and then edged carefully to the window to look down into the street.

There they saw Tiny Blue holding two sleek bay horses, plus a Winchester rifle. They saw the woman join him. Gracefully, each mounted into their saddles and raced out of town. The mud of the street kept any dust from flying and thus raising an outcry, as well as deadened the sound of hoofbeats.

The pair were well out of sight when one of the group in the crestfallen room above the Red Eye Saloon spoke.

"Who in the flaming hell was that, for Christ sake!"

"I got a notion," one of the group said.

He was an older man and when he said nothing further, one of his companions burst out angrily, "Well! Well, what the hell you gonna say. What's yer notion!"

"You know who she is, Charlie?" the third man asked.

"I ain't sayin' that," the man called Charlie said.

"Then what the hell are you sayin'!" demanded the man who had first expressed his anger.

"I bin thinking of Miller Rhodes," the older man named Charlie said.

"Miller Rhodes!"

"Why? What the hell has that got to do with this woman coming in here and robbin' us blind!"

"I dunno," Charlie said. "I dunno, but I just got reminded of Miller when she was here, and again like when we saw them two cutting out of town."

Chapter Four

Not very long after the much chastened cardsharps had soaked their sorrow over their humiliating treatment at the hands of the dark lady, the lady herself lay soaking in perspiration and the juices of lovemaking beneath her young husband. The time was the late afternoon, the setting the great outdoors of the Great American West.

They lay on a buffalo robe which the young husband always carried with him just for such a purpose, and now with great thrashing and gasping for air—which was plentiful all around them—they brought their rutting to a delirious climax.

Tiny Blue rolled off his glowing companion and lay on his back gazing up at the sun.

"Three times," the woman said. "That ought to hold us till we get to Blaze Rock." And she too squinted at the sun.

She was beautifully molded, with high, firm breasts, the big nipples of each were rosy, and she felt the tingling still from his sucking and chewing them. She had a long, flat belly, long legs, and high, firm, but not hard buttocks.

"C'mon, let's cut for Blaze Rock," she said, and she all but jumped to her feet.

Tiny Blue's dark eyes glowed as he watched her body flashing in the sunlight as she did a fast dance turn and curtsied to him.

"Thank you, kind sir, for your delicious lovemaking."

His penis began to stir once again as his eyes stroked her teats, her belly, her thighs between which nestled her dark, copious bush.

"I want some more," he said.

She pouted, mocking though, and wiggled her butt. "I am tired, sir. What the hell! We did it three times."

"Three good-fuck times," he said. "Four makes it even."

"Greedy! My man is greedy. My husband man!"

He grinned at her, his erection hard now. He was still lying on his back as she came closer, but this time with her mouth sliding onto his cock, while spreading her legs right over his face.

And they began their slow, undulating loving, while she moaned and he cried out with ecstasy, though because of his position, those cries were muffled.

Suddenly she spun around on top of him, and drove down onto his penis, sinking it into her soaking vagina. He cried out with the great joy of it. And now she began pumping up and down on his rigid member.

"I'm going to fuck you, my lad, like you've never been fucked before!" she hissed into his ear.

Tiny Blue was beyond speech. He simply lay there as she rode his stick up and down, around and around, and side to side; slowly, quickly, wiggling on it . . . until she finally was dripping with perspiration.

"Come . . . come!" Her tone was imperious, though she was gasping with her joy at the same time. "Come, my man! I demand that you come! I command thee to COME!" And with a gasping shriek she drove onto him rubbing the head of his cock right up into the center of everything in her . . . until she could bear it no longer, nor he . . . and they exploded into a mad series of convulsive comings.

They lay still.

Nearby their horses cropped the short buffalo grass. And the woman, whose name was Carisa Bolero, looked up at the sky and saw a bald eagle flying away. Had he been watching them, she wondered.

Carisa Bolero—an ageless beauty—lay somnolent beside her nineteen-year-old husband's snores which came evenly out of his deep sleep. Carisa had enjoyed many "husbands"—legitimate and otherwise—and she liked variety. Young, old, tall, short, Indian, white. She took them as she wished and on her own terms. With the exception of one.

She had met Miller Rhodes when she was sixteen and had fallen instantly under his sway. Miller was ten years older, and he was everything the young Carisa dreamed a man—her man—should be. From the little town of Upper Sandstone, where she had lived and they had met, they rode off into the westering sun and a life of highway robbery.

Miller was a top hand at his game. He knew everything it seemed, and he knew everyone he needed to know. He was "the best lover" Carisa ever had, to use her own words. They lived together, riding, drinking, lovemaking, robbing stages, banks, and anyone or anything else that came their way. Miller could boast of the most efficient gang of road agents in the West. The law couldn't lay a finger on him. He had a network of "friends" no matter where he threw his duffel, and it seemed he never made a mistake.

The youthful, though now experienced Carisa saw her life as a blissful experience; the permanent mistress of the great Miller Rhodes, and she exulted in the worship of her hero and his legend.

And then one day Miller and the boys rode off to one of their jobs, but returning to camp in their stead came a barreling crowd of angry and determined lawmen. Something had gone wrong—the inevitable "something." A bank teller had pulled a gun; there was shooting; the town rushed to action, and one member of the fabled Rhodes gang was captured; and under severe treatment gave away the whereabouts of the hideout.

The men of the law found Carisa, and dealt with her accordingly; that is to say, they questioned her endlessly. She remained firm. She knew nothing. She had never heard of Miller Rhodes, nor any road agent gang. She had been on her way to South Pass and had stumbled on the deserted camp. It took a while but she gained her freedom. But from then on she was on her own. As far as her life went, Miller Rhodes had disappeared. And she knew that her very presence with the law would keep him well away from her, for who knew who was following her about, waiting for her to team up with the bandit king again. From that day she started on her own career, still revering her idol, and waiting and longing for their reunion.

By this time Carisa found herself pregnant with Miller's child. And her joy was boundless when one night in Deadwood where she was staying at a cheap hotel, he slipped into her room. After a wild and miraculous night together he again took his departure, for the law was only moments away.

Following this bitter disappointment, Carisa spent time in what was for her honest employment. She dealt faro in a Fort Worth gambling house, played the piano when faro went slack, and all the while kidded with the customers with the customary raw, raucous humor of the frontier. And it was fun, too. For publicity purposes, the gambling house provided her with a high-stepping palomino, and when she wasn't dealing faro or playing the piano she rode around Fort Worth in a cowgirl outfit of buckskin and fringe and beads; its garishness emphasized by the twin six-guns at her hips.

Meanwhile, Miller had become so busy and was so constantly on the move that he could surely afford no dalliance with any female for more than a night or two, and surely not with a volatile jezebel such as the woman who by now had borne him a child. The child, whom Carisa had named Miller after the one and only man she really loved, carried her own surname— Bolero. She had left him with her family in Upper Sandstone.

Miller, along with a couple of members of his own gang, was now riding with the James and Younger boys, looting stages, banks, and trains.

The trail of the gang's enterprise in their chosen field lay strewn with more than a few dead, including three Pinkerton detectives. But then, at the very apex of their notoriety, the gang came a cropper when, possibly charmed by their publicity and the ease with which they had attained their great success, they went up against an enraged citizenry in attempting to rob three banks in one afternoon.

The pursuing posse killed three of the bandits and wounded and captured the rest, including Miller Rhodes. But it was not long before rumors began to circulate that Miller Rhodes had escaped, that he had shot his way out, bribed his jailers, or had been rescued by devoted followers of his exploits. Swiftly the stories developed into "hard fact," then legend. Miller had escaped the posse; he had shot his way out of prison; he had been rescued by friends; he was dead; and finally, one of the most attractive stories, that he had escaped and gone to South America. In any case, his activities had certainly diminished, and likeable rogue that he was, not a few mourned his passing from the lively Western scene.

Carisa believed all and none of the tales that came her way. Miller was alive in her heart and loins, and she began now to pile up money for his hoped-for return when she would take care of him. And in the event that he couldn't come to her, but needed money, she would have it to hand. Meanwhile, she had never been without male companionship for very long. Her latest amour, Tiny Blue, a dozen years her junior was a highly satisfactory consort. She had encountered him in a rough, wild region of the Indian Territory of Oklahoma. Part white and part Cherokee, he took up with her. As man and wife they roamed the country, but did not deign to suffer formal vows of marriage.

It was obvious to anyone with an eye that Tiny Blue

was wholly seduced into massive flattery by Carisa's amorous favors, with the result that his attitude towards her paralleled that of slave to mistress. On those occasions when she struck him with her riding whip, should he have incurred her displeasure, he accepted the punishment in silence.

On the other hand, with others he was a monster of uncontrolled violence, unless Carisa held him in. At rustling cattle she had never seen his equal, save of course for Miller her beloved, and it was in order to dispose of a stolen herd that the pair visited Shoshone and the Red Eye Saloon and Gambling Hall.

The cattle had fetched close to two thousand dollars, and while Carisa was pleased with the sum (for the moment) her eye fell suddenly on the gambling den a floor above the Red Eye, she was struck with an interesting way to increase their hard-earned funds.

It just so happened that Tiny Blue, though but still in his teens, was a shrewd poker player. However, following Carisa's instructions, he played the sucker and lost heavy amounts in the game, which he had swiftly seen to be crooked. Presently, with the sharps off guard and almost chortling at having—they thought—stripped a mug, Carisa entered the scene dramatically and at gunpoint collected not only Tiny Blue's two thousand but several thousand more.

Carisa, pleased with her enterprise, now planned to use it frequently. But ill luck struck again when Tiny, drinking without her one evening, killed a man in a fair fight, or so said the witnesses. The law saw otherwise and once again Carisa was manless.

She yearned desperately for Miller, whom she was

absolutely certain still lived. And now, by way of attracting him to her presence, and also as a means of adding to her Fund, should he need it, she embarked on a whole new enterprise. And to add sauce—which was always a Miller Rhodes touch—she launched her new career right in the Rhodes gang's old stamping grounds.

For the present, and to the relief of Cassius Wilfong and Wells Fargo, the bandits appeared to have taken a break in their brisk activities. There was no repetition of the train robbery, and only a minor stagecoach incident.

This occurred at Eagle Pass on the Billings run when a lone man suddenly appeared at the side of the trail and held up his hand for the stage to stop. It happened that the driver and guard were both new, and also young in experience (a grave oversight on the part of a lower echelon within the company) with the consequence that the guard, seeing the man with his hand raised, immediately ordered the driver to lay on the whip as he threw down the box with an oath, shouting, "Here's your goddamn box, goddamn yeh!" As the coach tore on its way through the pass, the driver flaying his horses and shouting at them, the passengers within fought to keep from mangling each other as they were thrown all around the coach.

It turned out that the man at the side of the road simply wanted a ride as a paying passenger, since his horse had gone lame and he'd had to shoot him.

Needless to say, this information when passed on to Cash Wilfong did nothing to improve that gentleman's feelings on the bandit situation.

Worse was in store, for suddenly, only a few days after this droll piece of action, the bandits began a fresh campaign against the stageline. This in itself was bad enough, but with the implication that they had been encouraged by the inefficiency, not to mention stupidity of the Wells Fargo guard, added bitter fuel to the fire burning hotly now in the superintendent who had vowed to "Get the bastards!"

At this point Wilfong had turned again to the Gunsmith.

"It's like I already told you, Clint. They're getting away not only with murder but all the gold, as fast as it gets mined! We have got to do something. I've tried everything. Extra men doesn't help. They've pulled off three quick ones this week alone!"

"I want to try something," Clint said. They were at the stage depot at Ranny's Point, where they had agreed to meet.

"Friend, you can try anything you want. I am at the end of it. I've run out my string. You've got a free hand. But do something. Shit, here I'd thought they'd cooled down, but they're worse than ever!"

"How are your men taking it?" Clint asked.

"Pretty hard. But it's like I told you last time, the bastards block the trail, I mean they're really forted up. My men can't even see who's firing at them."

"And what about the stage depots?"

"That's where they catch them changing horses."

"Bold, huh?"

"That they are."

"But recently they've been letting the depots alone."

Cash Wilfong nodded. "I've got my fingers crossed."

They fell silent a moment or so and then Clint said, "I've got something I want to try."

"By God, that's what I bin asking you, my lad!"

"It could cost a bit of money, but I want a free hand."

"All I can say to that is don't spare the hosses."

At the door Clint paused, adjusted his hat and looked closely at the Wells Fargo man. "Cash, I've got another question. Something besides what I have in mind as a first step."

"Shoot."

"You say they've not been hitting the stage depots."

Wilfong nodded. "Yeah. Like I said, they used to catch 'em when they're changing horses. But I think it's all right now, for the moment, since I put on extra men, and guns." He was watching the Gunsmith closely. "Why? You got something there?"

"Did they hit *all* the depots? Did they miss any?"

"Yeah . . . Well, I believe they passed up Drago Gulch. Course that could be on account of it's not a easy place to get in or out of, and not just for the Concord."

"Drago Gulch?"

"Other side of Eagle Pass."

"Who's the agent?"

Wilfong thought a moment. "Name's Cratcher, I believe." He sniffed. "Could be Thatcher or maybe Batcher. He's new. I'd have to look it up or check Glendenning on it. You got something?"

"Not yet. I want to try something first anyway."

And with a nod, touching two fingers to the brim of his hat, the Gunsmith opened the door and went out.

Cassius Wilfong let out a deep sigh. Reaching to his shirt pocket, he took out a fresh cigar and lit it.

He was damn glad to have Clint Adams working with him.

With the free hand given him by Wilfong, Clint went to work quickly. First he had one of the familiar big Glendenning Concord stages run into the shop in Billings, ostensibly for an overhaul. There, behind bolted doors and in strict secrecy, the Gunsmith directed a remarkable conversion.

The entire inside of the coach up to its windows was plated with iron tough enough to withstand the most powerful bullets. Masked gun ports were cut into all four sides. These were hinged so that they could be flipped open at a simple touch. The roof of the coach proper was also armored, and extra strong wheels were put in place of those formerly in use. The final effect was an armored coach, pulled by six horses. And yet, outwardly it looked no different than any other Glendenning stagecoach except that it rode more heavily on its thorough braces.

Finally—and this really appealed to the men working on the transformation—realistic dummies of a driver and shotgun guard were fastened on the box, and a set of fake reins were run from the end of the wagon tongue. The real driving was done from inside the coach, through a slit under the boot. Clint was figuring that when the Saddle City coach took the long Bonneville Grade and had to slow down, it would again be fair bait for the bandits, but since it would then be twilight, the deception had every chance of working, even at close range.

The night the job was finished, Clint had the driver, a veteran named Calvin Thumb put on a most believable drunk act for the citizens of Billings. Reeling from saloon to saloon he pounded down drink after drink—or appeared to—confiding to everyone that he was on a special run the next day, but that he was scared half to death because it was the biggest shipment ever; and he was sure the road agents would hit him. And when somebody asked him how Clyde Hendricks, his shotgun guard felt about it, Calvin replied that "Clyde, he is scared too, by God, too damn scared to take a drink tonight even, or even to go outside his cabin to take a leak. But me, Calvin Thumb, what the hell, me don't give a shit. Man can't live forever, dammit." And then he told anyone who was listening that they were sworn to secrecy!

The following day were there any doubters of Calvin's drunken gossip, they had only to see the heavy gray boxes with Wells Fargo stamped on them being loaded onto the afternoon stage. Calvin Thumb, looking like he'd had a big night, climbed carefully into his seat, and Clyde Hendricks got up onto the box with his shotgun. A muted cheer went up as the coach rattled down the street and onto the trail.

At a certain distance from the town, the regular stage swung off the road and up the bed of a dry wash. Around a bend a few hundred yards from the road, the armored coach was waiting, with its two dummies looking exactly like the real coach in the twilight.

Clint Adams was also waiting. "Wait here two hours," he told Thumb. "And then go on back to

Billings." He nodded to Hendricks the shotgun guard. "Get in here and join the boys."

There were two other armed guards crouching in the dark interior of the armored coach, along with the driver, and in a moment the Gunsmith joined them, making a cadre of five. A few minutes later the coach was rolling along the road to Saddle City; apparently the very same vehicle that had left Billings in full view of the crowd.

"You reckonin' they'll try an' stick us up?" a guard asked.

"I'm sure of it," the Gunsmith said. He grinned, "Fact, I'm hoping they will."

He had just said those words when the driver swore and seesawed on his reins bringing the heavy coach to a stop. They were in a narrow cut between jumbled masses of rock and just ahead of them a dead tree blocked the road.

A moment later a harsh voice called, "You on the box there, throw that shotgun over the side and get your hands up."

"Tell him to go to hell," Clint told Hendricks.

"Go to hell!" Clyde Hendricks shouted.

The reply was a thunderous blast of gunfire from the rocks. In the gloom, Clint counted at least six muzzle flashes, and heard the slugs thudding into the boot and the dummy figures above them.

There was silence then, and the querulous voice of one of the outlaws said, "What the hell? What's going on?"

"Now," the Gunsmith said inside the coach, his mouth close to Hendricks' ear, "fire where the flashes were."

"This is what's going on!" Clyde shouted as he flipped open his gunport and fired.

There was a yell of anguish, and the shadow by the rocks crumpled. Instantly the hidden bandits opened fire on the coach itself, and slugs hammered against the armor, which was doing its duty. Clint smiled grimly at that.

The guards, safe behind their bulletproof shields, returned the fire through the portholes.

Then Clint heard a whistle, and the firing stopped. The men inside the coach stopped firing too, for there were no gun flashes to aim at.

"The buggers have had enough," one of the guards said.

"We'll make sure." The Gunsmith's words were firm with caution.

Presently the men inside the armored coach heard a whistle and then the sound of hoofbeats dying away.

"They've gone," someone said.

"Wait," the Gunsmith said.

Only when he was certain that the road agents had fled did Clint give the signal to clamber out of the heated coach. They were all in much need of clear, fresh air.

The Gunsmith ordered them to move carefully just in case it was a trap.

Only a short distance off the road they discovered where the outlaws had rolled heavy rocks into a breastwork. They found no bodies, but there were puddles of blood on the ground, evidence that one or more of their shots had found a target.

Clint didn't follow the armored coach into Saddle City, but rode back to Prairie Falls. He was satisfied that the battle with the road agents had evened things. It should give spirit to Wells Fargo's shotgun riders, and certainly to Cash Wilfong.

As for the Gunsmith, as he rode through the night with Duke he kept remembering the whistle he'd heard calling off the bandit hostilities. He knew it had to be the same whistle he'd heard at the train robbery. And he now was also wondering where he'd heard the name Cratcher, even before Wilfong had mentioned it. The Wells Fargo superintendent hadn't been sure right at the moment whether the man who ran the stage depot at Drago's Gulch was Batcher or Cratcher, or just what, but Clint knew the name Cratcher. He still couldn't recollect where he'd heard the name, but he did know he didn't have a very good feeling associated with it.

Chapter Five

Tiny Blue—though but nineteen years, was a young man of infinite resource and managed to escape prison. Had he remained for his trial he surely would have reaped a most severe sentence at the harsh hands of Judge Isaac Parker—famed as "The Hanging Judge." Tiny's jailer, a kindly gentleman, made the fatal mistake of allowing his prisoner to have a visitor. The visitor, an old lady claiming to be the "poor boy's aunt," brought him a pie made of apple, crust and a very sharp knife.

Discovering the knife that "Auntie" Carisa had baked in her apple pie, Tiny called his jailer and dutifully reported the infraction of rules. The jailer, one Art Delehanty, had never run into such an honest prisoner, and was shocked to the point where he took his attention completely off his youthful charge—he'd been staring bug-eyed at the vicious-looking knife— just long enough for Tiny to knock him cold with one punch, delivered right onto his left eardrum.

The next thing jailer Delehanty knew was that he was lying on the floor with the room spinning around him. He came to his senses slowly; finally with alarm charging through him he sat up. He was alone in the cell with the door locked from the outside, minus his keys, minus the knife that his prisoner had shown him, and what was more, minus even the apple pie.

Meanwhile, out on the trail, Tiny Blue and "Auntie" Carisa were riding briskly towards their next adventure, having hungrily finished off the pie that they'd had the foresight to bring along with them.

Clint Adams had awakened early in his room at the Junction House, and this morning, rather than having breakfast in the hotel dining room, he had decided to try one of the three cafés in town. He settled on the Rock Café, and was intrigued to find that while the small establishment was not run by one of Clint Fiddle's brothers, it was nevertheless owned and operated by the widow of Clarence Fiddle, the brother Clinton had said "up and died on us."

Meg Fiddle was a broad-beamed lady with an expressive face. Clint instantly read her as a first-rate gossip, and so he went out of his way to encourage her. He didn't have to try very hard. Meg was even more garrulous than her brother-in-law Clancy at the Hard Dollar.

"You be that Gunsmith feller," she said right off. "Heard about you. They tell me you're quickern' a pissed rattler. That so?"

She leaned on the counter, her huge bosom pushing against her calico dress. "Don't tell me," she went on. "I got no business askin' such a thing. Only thing is, in this town a man—a woman too—has got to know who's with 'em, an' who be against."

"Got'cha," Clint said, stirring sugar into his cup of coffee.

Meg turned, helped herself to a cup of coffee, and then turned back to her customer. They were the only ones in the café, and Clint realized that the woman wanted to try pumping him. He wondered why. Was it because she was simply curious, nosey? Or was she trying to get a line on him for somebody else?

"I heard about the stage trick you pulled on the road agents," she went on. Her voice rich with the invitation to gossip, her eyes fully on him now, like dark berries, claiming information that he alone could give her.

Clint had decided to be just a little open with her, as open as he could be without compromising anything.

"Seems news travels no matter where you go," he said genially.

"Well, you don't look like a owl hooter; and you don't look like a card mechanic; and though I reckon you've moren' likely punched your share of cows, you don't look like you just come in with a trail herd." She shrugged elaborately, her heavy bosom bouncing as she did so. "So that leaves the law. An' there ain't no star, 'less you wear it in your pocket." She sniffed. "That leaves the mines. But you don't have the look. Only thing left is regulating for the cattlemen or the stage line or Wells Fargo." She put down her cup of coffee and placed both hands wide on the counter and leaned, thus bringing her shoulders up around her ears.

"You left out schoolteacher."

"That's women."

"How about preacher?"

She wagged her heavy head from side to side. "Too much fun in your face for that one."

"You forgot the real one."

"Maybe I never knew it."

"Gunsmith."

"Guns. Well, that's the way it goes. Not that it's any of my business, mister, and I ain't breathin' a word. Only tryin' to talk real friendly like to a good looking stranger who looks like he could give a honest woman a real good time."

At this delivery Clint felt an alarm going off inside him. The big woman standing before him, could only be a source of information as far as he was concerned—if that. Nothing more. But his alarm grew as she rolled her seductive eyes over his face and chest.

"You've got me wrong," he said swiftly, trying to keep his voice steady in the wake of Meg Fiddle's growing lechery. "I am actually a gunsmith by trade. I repair guns—fix, rebuild them. I don't happen to have my gunsmith wagon with me right now, but I'm still in the market for work. Maybe you've got a gun in need of repair?"

She was staring at him, her eyes as big as apples. "Jesus . . . if that don't beat all." She ran the back of her wrist under her nose, sniffed, and reached for her coffee. "Here I went an' figgered you for a Wells Fargo, or one of them regulators for the mines, somethin' like that. An' I sure as hell 'pologize, bein' as how it ain't the custom of the country to ask personal questions; not that it's my usual way anyways, mister, exceptin' I just kind of liked the cut of your rig, if you follow what I mean. And I sure do 'pologize. The coffee's on me. An' by the way, my name's Meg."

"My name is Clint."

They smiled at each other, and Clint decided that he liked her; only remembering abruptly her sexual acquisitiveness and her total lack of appeal to him, he became serious.

"Ever hear of a place called Drago Gulch," he asked mildly.

"Up round Eagle Pass."

"They've got a stage depot I hear, and I was figuring to cover some of the depots if they aren't too far away, to see if there might be some gun work I could do."

She looked straight at him. "Gun fixin' you're meaning."

Clint nodded. "Just like I told you. I'm considered good at my trade."

"I do believe they got some depot or line camp or somethin' up there by the Gulch, but you better ask somebody else on that. I'm a town body. I don't know much about the trail."

And with that she turned and picked up her cup and walked into the kitchen.

"Can I have another coffee," Clint called out after a minute had passed.

She came back out of the kitchen then, and without looking at him, picked up his cup and carried it out for a refill. When she came back with it she still kept her eyes averted.

Clint was about to say something when the door of the café opened and two men entered.

They nodded at the woman behind the counter,

took a quick look at Clint Adams and sat down at the far end of the counter, as far away from him as they could get. At this point Meg Fiddle caught his eyes.

"You could try the Rimrock," she said in a loud voice. "Or the Junction House. Strangers mostly find it's an even toss between the two."

Her eyes were sharp with caution as she looked at Clint now, placing those words carefully in his awareness.

"I'm already at the Junction House," Clint said, picking up on her message. "But just thought I'd ask what else there was in town."

Meg Fiddle had turned to her two new customers now, though not before passing Clint another look that read "be careful."

"Coffee all round here," said the bigger of the two men.

They were both big, and both wore tied-down six-guns, one on his right thigh, the other on his left.

"Sure you wanta stay in here, Burt?" said the one nearest Clint. "I mean, Meg here's sure losin' business. Eh, Meg?" he called out to the kitchen.

His companion joined him now, in a voice that seemed to come from the bottom of his chest. "I'd sure say business was bad when you look at the kind of trash you're taking in." His cold eyes were dead on Clint Adams as he spoke.

Clint felt the slight pressure in his chest, then the loosening as he watched the two men. They were grinning, very sure of themselves.

"You boys behave yourselves now," Meg said, coming from the kitchen with their coffee. "This here is a stranger, and he was just askin' me where things are in town."

Clint could see the little pulse beating in her neck as she spoke, and his feelings went out to her. She had courage. He stood up.

"Boys, I'm just leaving. Enjoy your coffee."

He had started to the door when suddenly the man nearest him was off his stool and standing right in front of him, barring his way.

"Go out the back, mister." And he jerked his thumb in the direction of the kitchen.

Meg had started toward the kitchen.

"Where you think you're goin'!" the man who was still seated at the counter snapped.

"My soup's boiling over."

"Leave it!" he nodded to the Gunsmith. "Out the back, you!"

As Clint stepped into the kitchen he heard the other man say, "You bitch! What you bin talkin' to him about!"

"I told you. Nothin' except some of the places in town, like the Junction House and the Rimrock."

Clint heard the slap as it hit her and her cry. Quickly he stepped to the stove, picked up the pot of boiling soup, and hurried into the front room and threw it right at the man who had hit Meg Fiddle.

As the boiling soup covered him the man screamed. His companion jumped off his stool, slapping leather, but his hand never reached his gun grip before the Gunsmith smashed the heavy metal pot right into his face, knocking him over backwards as he tripped on the leg of one of the stools. Meanwhile, the man who had been scalded was cursing in pain and anger. As he stood weaving in the middle of the floor, the Gun-smith plucked his six-gun from its holster, then did the same to his companion who was struggling to his feet.

"You special gents can go out the front door," he said. "It's quicker, and besides, you won't be stinking up the kitchen."

He shoved them out the door, then standing in the doorway he broke each gun open and smashed it on the stone doorstep.

The first to recover was the one who'd been hit with the empty pot. "You son of a bitch, I'll get you!"

"Not with this gun you won't," said the Gunsmith, stepping out into the street. "But bring it around for repair. I might fix it for you, if the price is right. Tell your boss, huh? Both of you, be sure to tell your boss how you handled things this day."

He walked back into the café now and sat down in the same seat he'd sat in before.

"I'll take that second cup of coffee now, Mrs. Fiddle."

It wasn't only Wells Fargo and Superintendent Cassius Wilfong who was hurting from the vigorous depredations of the "new outlaws"—as the gang became known, or was it gangs? The whole of the northern country—the gold fields—felt the yoke of oppression. Always attendant to any journey was the likelihood of hostilities. No traveler was safe, no Wells Fargo box seemed to escape. And of course, high on the list of victims were the stagecoaches themselves, their drivers and shotgun guards. And perhaps most colorfully "Big Bob" Glendenning himself, owner and architect of the Glendenning Stage Line, which ran mostly in the goldfield country, but also having runs as far away as Buffalo Rock, Butte, and Cheyenne. But it was, of course, the goldfield run that was at the core of Big Bob's anger.

As a consequence of the bind he had conferred with Wells Fargo—in the person of Cash Wilfong—and together they had decided to join forces.

Clint Adams was aware of this arrangement as he rode north on his way to Drago Gulch. Wilfong had filled him in on the situation between Glendenning and the company, as he called Wells Fargo.

Now, riding north on the way to Eagle Pass and Drago Gulch, the scene with Wilfong returned to Clint—how Cash had unburdened himself on his concern at losing the company's money, and how glad he was to have Clint at hand, plus the fact that he was also allied with Glendenning.

"But you're allied with him anyway, aren't you?" Clint had asked.

"Sure. Wells Fargo is always with the transport company, no matter what line it is, and also of course the railroad, But Glendenning's a tough old bird, one of those go-it-himself types. And, you know, the kind of man that builds an empire all by himself just about, doesn't mind blaming the hell out of Wells Fargo for having his driver's and hosses shot up, and passengers manhandled to boot."

"In your spot, Cash, you get it coming and going, don't you," Clint had said with a wry grin.

Yet now, riding through the tall spruce and pine with the azure sky twinkling through the tops of the trees, and the rich smell of the timber all around him,

he recalled Wilfong's telling him how Glendenning
had been sympathetic toward the express company,
and had not harangued Wells Fargo and Cash as he
had in the past. Clint knew that his friend Cash could
take care of himself. The superintendent had handled
men like Big Bob Glendenning in the past, and indeed
had handled him in the present trouble.

As he broke out of the stand of timber now, Clint
grinned to himself. He'd known Cash Wilfong a good
while, from back in the days when the man was a
simple—though by no means ordinary—range detec-
tive.

Now, free of the tall trees, the great bowl of sky
swam overhead as he walked Duke out onto the top of
the rimrock, his vision caught by the magnificent
snowcapped mountain peak that had so suddenly
come into view.

He had not lost his awareness—he never lost his
trail attention—yet he felt his breath catch almost like
a blow as he looked at the white mountain top, framed
in the endless blue sky. And beyond, he wondered
suddenly. Were there others? And beyond those?

At the same time his attention was present, and so
he did not permit himself to get lost.

"Eh, Duke," he said softly to the big black horse.
And he reached down and ran his fingers through the
gelding's thick mane, right in front of his stock saddle
where the edge of his Navajo blanket was raised.

His clear, searching eyes now washed across the
morning sky, moving down to the layers of mountains
on the horizon, then closer down to the long, wide
valley sweeping below, with the river racing through

cottonwood and box elder, swollen and surely roaring, though he was too far away to hear it.

The Gunsmith waited another moment, his eyes still searching. There a band of elk grazing, there a lone coyote, and over there a jay starting from a clump of bullberry bushes. Something had startled it. And then, so far below, he saw the stage coming, a tiny dot tumbling along behind its six-horse team. The driver was laying on the whip, the shotgun messenger holding on, his gun probably under his legs so he could hold with both hands to the rocking coach, for there was no danger in sight—either red or white that the Gunsmith could see.

He had taken out his field glasses now and was watching the coach as it charged across the floor of the valley, a great wall of dust rising behind it, then softening into a loose cloud and finally disappearing into the day. They were really cutting along, faster than necessary it seemed to Clint. For the passengers inside the coach had to be having a helluva time keeping their seats.

As the stagecoach and horses came closer to his vision, Clint saw that there was a passenger on the roof along with the baggage. He was holding on for his life, spread-eagling his legs, and with one hand gripping some rope or baggage—it wasn't clear. His other hand was apparently free, for at one moment he reached up to press his hat further down onto his head. Clint couldn't see for sure, but he had the definite impression that the man riding on the top of the coach was holding something in his free hand. He only needed one guess on that, he told himself as he lifted his reins and turned Duke back toward the trail.

Whatever it was going on down there, it was much too far away, and the action was going too fast for him to be able to do a damn thing about it.

As he rode now, his thoughts turned again to the two toughs who had braced him in Meg Fiddle's café. They had obviously known who he was, though his name hadn't been mentioned. Yet they had that familiarity about them—their gestures, their faces, the way they moved and the intonation of their voices.

In any case, Meg Fiddle had known them, or known who they were.

"They're from the Crossbones outfit, and they hang out up by Drago Gulch; and funny you was askin' me about the Gulch just before."

"You know them."

She shook her head; she was still sweating from the encounter. "I don't know 'em. I know who they are. They bin in here before. Caused trouble last time too. Beat up on a boy, a kid. They're scum. I seen 'em comin' through the window, and that's why I started talkin' different to you so quicklike."

"I appreciate it," the Gunsmith said seriously. "It did help, warning me like that."

He had been sitting at the counter as she'd brought another mug of coffee. "Tell me who this Crossbones outfit is," he said. "Is that real bones, or somebody's name."

"It is real bones, and probably human, judging by the kind of men they got there. They don't come to Junction often, but whenever they do it's a happy time when they take a notion to leave. Word is a lot of those boys throw a wide loop."

"They got a head man?"

"I hear so, but I dunno who. They tell me—I mean, what I hear around town—and not askin' but just hearin', mind you—I hear that there is more than one bunch of hard cases out there. So I dunno if it's all run by the same pair of hands."

"At Drago Gulch."

"No. Not exactly. I mean according to what I heard. The bunch, they're s'posed to be north of the Gulch, almost up by Buffalo Basin." She mopped her brow. "I just sure hope they don't come back."

"Do you think they will?"

"I dunno. I don't see how they can figger I helped you any."

"They were looking for me," Clint had said.

"You mean, like already before they come in here?"

He nodded. "Someone set 'em on me."

Her lips were round with surprise. "Holy God to that!" And she crossed herself, her eyes suddenly loaded with faith.

"I really don't think they'll come back here," Clint said, looking seriously at her. "You didn't throw boiling water at them and hit them with a heavy pot."

"If the buggers come back here I'll have me husband's Henry with me. Got it at home, and I always keep it by my bed. I'll start packin' it to me work, I will."

And with that the Gunsmith had left her. He really didn't believe those two toughs would come back. But they could very well pay him a visit at the Junction House, or lay for him in an alley or along the trail.

Now, fleetingly as he cantered after the coach, he was thinking of the pair, wondering if he would perhaps run into them at Drago Gulch. On the other hand, he was well aware that he could be climbing the wrong tree. In any case, he decided, whether or not he ran into the two toughs, he wanted to visit Drago Gulch, that is, the depot. Indeed, he wanted to check all the depots on the stage run, where horses were changed, and meals were served. But especially he wanted to visit Drago Gulch depot, for he had heard of Cratcher, remembering more of him now. He had heard a good deal about Cratcher and he wondered why such a man as Big Bob Glendenning would hire such a man to manage one of his stations.

He was riding just below the crown of a long, high ridge now, not silhouetted against the skyline and in fact well covered, yet with a good view of the sweep of land all the way down to the river. Then he saw the dots moving along the edge of some cottonwoods. They must have just forded the river, for he could see water glistening under the sunlight along the horses' legs as they moved along in single file.

A hunting party? It could be. They didn't look hostile, but you couldn't really tell from this distance.

He had planned to ride down along the bank of the river, but now wisely decided on a different trail. Why take a chance like that after all. He was collecting enough trouble as it was. He didn't need Indian trouble.

Clint Adams knew a good bit about Big Bob Glendenning, and he appreciated Cash Wilfong's enthusiasm at having him as an ally in the struggle with the road agents, rather than an adversary who blamed his losses—which were a whole lot less than Wells Fargo's—on the express company. Clint suspected that there was more to Glendenning's amiability and "cooperation" than appeared to the casual eye. Not that he suspected the stagecoach king of any impropriety, but he was carefully holding his view of the situation in reserve.

He had heard what a taskmaster Glendenning was, and how he ran his company right to the finest detail—the quality of horses, their harness, the behavior of his station agents, everything. In fact, it was known how men sometimes chided Glendenning for spending so much money on matched teams when common horseflesh was so cheap.

Big Bob's answer was classic. "Did you ever take a good look at an Indian pony? Runty and starved half to death on bunch grass. Listen, the day my teams can't outrun an Indian war party, I'm out of business."

And he was as stubbornly individualistic in his manner of choosing men. He wanted the roughest, the toughest, the most able in the whole of the West. And that's what he got.

The few rules Bob set were rigidly enforced. Being drunk on the box, being rude or disrespectful to a passenger or swearing beyond the normal need under trying circumstances in their role as drivers brought instant dismissal. Big Bob was tough, but he was fair.

He ruled the roads—at least in that section of the West where his coaches traveled. But it became necessary that he had to rule the depots and even some of the one-horse towns that sprang up around those stopping places where horses were changed, meals were served and the passengers could stretch their legs and loosen their behinds.

The tale-tellers had it that when Big Bob hired Thor Cratcher he told him he wanted him for his division manager, and he could start by riding over to Prairie Falls and Junction which, since the absence of Miller Rhodes and his gang of unbelievable gunslingers, had sunk into a den of total iniquity; a veritable nest of violence run by a brute named Kodl.

According to the tale-tellers—notably in Clint's case, the loquacious Clancy Fiddle—Cratcher had said to Big Bob, "You're saying you want me to clean up Junction and get rid of that son of a bitch Kodl." To which it is reliably reported that Mr. Glendenning replied, "Do it any way you want, but do it."

The encounter between Cratcher and Kodl became instant legend. The men met on the street that ran through the middle of Prairie Falls and Junction with bullets lacing the air between them. The inhabitants of that rugged hamlet had vanished. Both men went down badly wounded. But before losing consciousness on the wooden boardwalk outside the Moosehead Saloon, Cratcher managed to leave a message. "Tell the son of a bitch I'll be back to finish the job."

It took Cratcher nearly four months to recover. He was in a great deal of pain the while. His adversary had recovered sooner. But Cratcher's pain apparently brought him into a state of violence that simply had to be assuaged.

According to report, he found Kodl drinking in a saloon, chased him out into the street, and for a mile out of town before catching him. There he tied Kodl to a fence post and for the remainder of the day he shot his victim again and again in nonfatal spots. Finally, he had Kodl begging for mercy, begging Cratcher to kill him. Cratcher, however, was in no great hurry. He took his time, waiting till sundown before delivering the ultimate bullet to his prisoner. Then he cut off both of Kodl's thumbs and took them as souvenirs.

Apparently this was sufficient to pass Big Bob's qualifications for a division manager.

Clint Adams had heard the story about Cratcher before, listening to it again from Clancy Fiddle. He knew some people had been horrified by the tale, and everyone agreed that it surely revealed the character of Mr. Cratcher.

The Gunsmith agreed with that, but he was much more interested in how the tale disclosed the character of Bob Glendenning.

Chapter Six

The Gunsmith had sized the situation with absolute accuracy. The racing stagecoach he had seen through his field glasses was indeed moving too fast for him to do anything about it. And so was the action on top of the coach which was urging the driver to whip his team into a foaming gallop.

Tiny Blue inched forward carefully, holding onto the manila rope which lashed the baggage to the roof of the coach. He was nimble, also young and healthy, and he loved the action. Probably it was in his blood, the Cherokee portion. Even so he was having a rough time staying on top of the racing coach while still ordering the driver and guard with his handgun.

"Faster!" And he poked the barrel of the big Navy Colt into the driver's spine, then pointed it at the shotgun messenger beside him. "We'll make Drago anytime now," he said.

"By God, ye'll have Cratcher to deal with there, my lad," snarled the driver, and to emphasize his words he cracked the whip expertly over the heads of the lead team.

"Cratcher—huh!" Tiny Blue chuckled. "Cratcher ain't goin' to be there." He grinned. He had a tooth missing in the upper front row. His dark liquid eyes felt along the trail ahead. He was still grinning. Nothing. Carisa had seen to that. For a woman she really knew how to handle things—guns, horses, the gang of riders. Well, good. And he, he knew how to handle her. He almost chuckled aloud as he thought of her demands on him. Well he came up with it, and even wanted more. And, by damn the woman was always willing! Never got tired of it! Never!

Suddenly the coach gave a bad lurch and he almost lost his balance. Better watch that! Thinking about the woman could land him with a broken neck or worse. Pay attention!

Looking ahead now he saw the line of timber which fringed the edge of the stage depot. They were almost there. He was sure hoping there hadn't been any slipups from the woman's end. But there wouldn't be. That woman knew what she was doing. A woman you could count on. Not like some!

They were in the trees now, and it was suddenly cooler as the driver slowed his team.

"Keep 'em moving," Tiny Blue said.

"They'll founder, God Dammit!" snapped the man with the lines. He was an old-timer.

Tiny didn't push him.

"Only while we're in the timber here. When we hit daylight again you skin 'em!"

The driver spat a streak from his chew, started to say something, then held his tongue. The guard meanwhile sat in raging silence. Seeing daylight up ahead as they rolled through the cathedral of tall trees, Tiny Blue felt a surge of excitement.

And then they were in the clear, bursting out of the

trees, the driver laying on the whip at Tiny's swift command, and prod from the Colt.

And then something all the way inside him bounced as he saw them! The two horsemen, one on each side of the trail sitting still on good horseflesh, each with a rifle at the ready. By damn, the woman had sure done her part!

"Son of a bitch!" It was the guard speaking for the first time since Tiny Blue had braced them.

"They ain't takin' no chances," snapped the driver.

Ahead lay the long, wide slope at the bottom of which stood the log cabin depot. Behind it a big corral with fresh horses waiting, ready to be hooked up to the shafts of the coach.

"Don't see what the hell yer hurry is," the driver grumbled. "Here's more of yer welcoming committee."

"Just makin' sure," Tiny Blue said.

"Wonder what happened to Cratcher," the guard said as a half dozen horsemen appeared from the other side of the log cabin.

"That is a dumb question," said the driver.

"I wouldn't say that. Cratcher ain't the kind to be bamboozled by a bunch of half-assed owl hooters. I figure he's got to be away, like maybe out hunting."

"Pull up," Tiny said.

"What the hell you think I'm doin'!" the driver snapped, sawing on his long lines.

They came to a foaming stop, the driver pulling on the brake and the riders, all heavily armed, surrounded the coach.

"Get down and open the door and get them passengers out and lined up," Tiny ordered as he holstered the big Navy Colt and climbed nimbly down from his perch.

He stood there, scratching his crotch, grinning at the passengers as they got down from the coach and lined up. Then one of the gunmen stepped forward with his hat in his hand.

"Put all your valuables in the hat," Tiny Blue said. And he giggled, looking at a young woman who was obviously terrified.

She was cute, maybe in her early twenties, or maybe younger. Blond, wide-set eyes and a bust which her high-necked dress set off beautifully and—Tiny Blue began to feel—maddeningly. He took a step forward.

"That is enough," The sharp voice directly behind him was like a knife. The blow on the back of his head from the riding crop almost knocked him off balance. The second blow, on the side of his neck and face did. He went to his knees, reaching up slowly toward his bleeding cheek.

"Do you want more!"

She was standing before him, her crop ready for another blow.

"I said! . . ."

"No—no more!"

"Please! Please no more!" She was mimicking his voice, but with pleading, begging in the tones.

"Please! Please no more!"

"You little son of a bitch, get inside! Right now! Git!"

As he struggled to his feet, she kicked him, almost knocking him down. He staggered, maintaining himself more or less upright.

"Lucky I don't kick you someplace else!"

She did not deign to watch him slinking off to the cabin, but turned her attention to the stage passengers. Everyone present had all but frozen under the drama of the amazing scene. Three men, two women, the driver and shotgun messenger.

"Go on now. Fill the hat. We are hardworking bandits, and we need the money for our mothers and daddies, our wives and husbands, and of course our dear, sweet, adorable babies and small children. Goddamit!" she burst out suddenly, her face scarlet with anger. "Hurry it up! We don't have all day!"

The outlaws broke into movement now. One man signaled the stage driver who moved towards the horses and began unhitching them.

"Get those teams changed," said the woman, cool again.

Meanwhile, two men had got the box down from the boot, and brought it to where the woman was standing. They stepped away.

Then, with one flowing movement, the woman who was dressed in a man's outfit—black pants, black shirt, a Mexican buscadero carrying her twin guns, took a step forward at the same time that her left hand stroked smoothly to her hip, drew the six-gun and fired. Without even the space of a breath, she reholstered that wholly accurate weapon and looked at one of her men.

"Open it."

The man sprang to obey.

"Now load the horses and we'll move out. One of you get him." And she nodded in the direction Tiny Blue had gone.

In a moment more, the fresh team of horses had been brought from the corral and hitched to the coach. Then two men had mounted their horses and hazed the original team of six horses almost out of sight, scattering them along the way. When they returned, Tiny Blue and his mistress were mounted, as were all the other riders.

The passengers had remained silent, awestricken actually, in the light of Tiny Blue's disciplining. That gentleman was quite composed as the bandits rode off. He rode just behind his lady who was now smoking a cigar, while behind them the coach and six-horse team rumbled along.

At a good distance from the stage depot Carisa held up her arm, signaling a stop.

"Unhitch them here," she ordered. "Then flip the coach over." She waited, without a word to her escort, whose face now showed a large black and blue welt. Yet, Tiny Blue's eyes were shining. For he could feel her. God, she was like an animal, he thought.

The men overturned the heavy coach, and with further instructions from their leader, they mounted their horses and headed back to their camp in the rocks.

Carisa and her escort rode together. After a while, when she was convinced nobody could possibly be following, the two found a secluded area off the trail. Tiny Blue spread the robe he always brought along for such occasions, and in only moments they were locked in embrace.

"I wanted to do it in the coach," she said.

"We could of."

"I mean while it was being driven."

"Close your eyes," he said. "And I'll drive you."

"Let me turn over. I want it on my hands and knees, you son of a bitch."

"Come on," he said.

"That little bitch was young enough to be your kid sister."

Tiny Blue wanted to say that the girl was young enough to be his partner's daughter. Only he didn't dare. And as he thrust his erection into her spread vagina, mounting her from the rear, nothing was in him that wished in any way to endanger his great pleasure.

When the Gunsmith reached the depot at Drago Gulch he found the stage passengers in a turmoil. The stage driver and his guard had gone out on foot to try to catch one of the horses so that they could wrangle in the rest. Clint hadn't spotted the horses as he'd ridden in, and so he reasoned that they were gone in another direction. His opinion was verified when someone told him that the bandits had pushed the horses towards the mountain which rose behind the flat land at the bottom of the long coulee that led into the depot.

At the same time, while the passengers were in a turmoil at being delayed on their journey, they were managing. The two women had gone through the log house locating something in the way of food. One of the men had built a fire in the kitchen range. The remaining two men passengers were telling each other how they were going to complain to the company about the rotten service.

It didn't take Clint very long to locate the horses. Luckily they were bunched together, and he wrangled them back to the depot well before dark. Then, following the tracks left by the bandits, he found the coach. By the time he got the men out there with the horses, it was nearly dark.

They were all hot, excited now upon their return, and the women laid on a good supper.

There was still no sign of the division manager. No Cratcher.

"They might of taken care of Cratcher," the driver said to Clint in a low voice so the passengers wouldn't hear. "Dumped him someplace. Wouldn't put it past the bastards."

"Funny him being not here," the guard said. "Big Bob, he is a stickler for business being run just so."

"It's fixing to rain," the Gunsmith said, putting down his plate of food.

"Are you saying that we'll not go on tonight, Mr. Adams?" It was the youthful blond girl, who had so attracted Tiny Blue. Two of the men had related the episode to the Gunsmith with relish. The two women had been silent.

"I think it best not to, miss," Clint said, taking in her fine looking figure, her color that had suddenly filled her cheeks as he turned his attention to her, and—yes, he was pretty sure of this—her special intake of breath. He liked her eyes, her eyebrows, and the tilt of her nose, not to mention the rest of her. Especially when she bent down to retrieve a fork that had fallen from the table at which they had been having supper.

The other woman released a sigh. She was older

than the girl, wore a wedding band, and in fact had told the company she was joining her husband in the goldfields where he had "struck it rich." Her eyes had flashed as she said this.

The men passengers immediately started a poker game following supper, while the women withdrew to what was evidently the depot manager's bedroom. Clint decided to take a look at Duke and the other horses. He was aware of his own uneasiness. It was certainly not the moment to fall asleep. And there was still no sign of Cratcher.

It had started to rain lightly. The drops were thin, falling not of their own volition but as though released from the mist that had slipped silently into the valley. The drops were soon even less formed, and it seemed, they were hardly even wet. When Clint Adams walked out to the corral to check on Duke it was as though only the air itself was wet, and he had the feeling that soon the sky would clear.

He wondered why he was feeling uneasy. There was surely no likelihood that the road agents would return. They had no reason for a second pass. They had the contents of the box and also the passengers' valuables. The question he had now was whether it was the same gang that he had seen at the holdup of the train at Moose River. Had the leader been the woman then? It could have been. The figure he had seen was slender, only then there had been no showing off like that described by the passengers at the depot. At the train, everything had been quite correct, although from what he gathered, the woman's actions at the depot had been sparked with jealousy. And he knew very well that jealousy could make a fool out of the toughest outlaw.

But what had happened to Cratcher? Was he in cahoots with the gang, and had taken off simply to allow them a free hand, and avoid implication for himself? It seemed so.

Thus, the woman and Cratcher would be working together? Strange, he reflected now, as he leaned against the side of the corral, listening to the horses, to the land, the dying night. Strange—yes, the woman. He had not heard of such a person. But what was interesting was that if it was the same bandit leader as the one at the train then something very interesting was revealed.

First of all, a leader of a gang who was coldly alert, planned everything with extreme care, covered all the possibilities and worked with no unnecessary excitement or showing off. In a word, a leader with a steel grip on the men and all aspects and possibilities in a holdup situation.

But in the second holdup—at the stage depot—here was a leader who revealed herself. While the men wore masks, except the half-breed, the woman did not. Furthermore, she allowed herself to indulge in jealousy. And so why did he think it was the same gang, the same leader? There was absolutely no evidence for that. The only thing that was present to both holdups was himself who actually hadn't been that much on the spot the second time.

Yet the hunch nagged at him. What were the similarities? Boldness right off struck him. And ease. Both events had been colorfully done. The train holdup with underplaying, the stage job almost on the

order of a show, a circus. Even running the stage off
and turning it over had been something on the order of
showing off. Why?

Checking back now with gossip and information he
had gathered in and around Prairie Falls, he had the
definite impression that there had been various holdup
gangs, but one main one. That main one had the
reputation of acting with strictness regarding behavior
and care in relation to the passengers and stagecoach
handlers such as the driver and shotgun messenger,
unless of course the moment called for disciplinary
action. And even then, the reprisals—he had heard—
were executed with neatness and dispatch. And so,
once again, why did he feel the woman bandit leader
was also the leader of the train holdup that he had
witnessed?

He knew there was no reason for this notion. It
made no sense. Still, it stayed with him. There was
something. Of that he was sure. He felt it all the way
through him now, as he turned and walked around to
the corral gate.

Ten minutes later he had led Duke out of the corral
and saddled and bridled him. He had just led the horse
over to the cabin when the door opened and someone
came outside. There was no light, but the sky had
cleared now and the moon was there. He stopped,
listening to his surroundings. And while he stood
there, wholly alert, the figure came toward him. It
was the young woman, the blonde with the wide-set
green eyes and the high bosom.

"Can't sleep?" Clint said. "It's a good idea to get
as much rest as you can."

"I doubt a horse could sleep in there the way those

men are snoring," she said, but her tone was light, even humorous. "Are you leaving us?"

"I think you can handle yourselves tomorrow," he said. "The road agents won't be back."

She stood straight in front of him now, and then lifted her head to look at the moon. Her eyes returned to him. "Are you from these parts, Mr. Adams? I hope you don't mind my asking, but I am going to Prairie Falls—looking for someone actually."

"You want to know if I know the person."

She nodded. "I'm looking for my sister. I haven't seen her since, well for some years—since she left home, back in Pennsylvania. Five, six years ago. I was quite young then, and anyway I'm looking for her."

"She's not expecting you?" Clint asked, suddenly interested. He had a good feeling about the girl. He could tell she was soft. There was an openness in her voice, which he didn't find very often in meeting people along the trail. She was not guarded. Maybe she was younger than he had thought.

"No, she isn't expecting me. In fact, I am not certain how she will be when and if I do find her." She gave a small laugh.

She was clearly nervous, and he liked her for that. Her simplicity was touching.

"Actually, I'm just visiting Prairie Falls, so I'm not much acquainted."

"Oh."

She had moved closer and so had he. And now he could feel her presence strongly, like a movement through the atmosphere between them.

"I'll keep my ears open if that's any help to you,"

he said. "I expect to be in town a bit, though not for very long. But you'll likely see her. It's a small town. It doesn't take more than half a day to see about everybody in Prairie Falls."

She gave a little laugh at his joke. "I'm not sure my sister's really there, and I surely don't know how she will receive me. I can only hope."

He started to turn toward his horse. "Well, tell me her name, just in case I hear something."

"Melanie. Melanie Lansing."

The Gunsmith had a sudden notion that he'd heard that name before somewhere, but he had no time to think on it. At that very moment Duke whiffled low in his long nose, and from the other side of the corral Clint heard a bit jangle.

"Get inside," he said quickly to the girl. "Fast!"

And as she hurried back to the cabin, he pulled the Winchester out of its scabbard that was attached to his saddle. He heard the other horse and rider now as he stationed himself at a corner of the house by a water barrel. He could see the corral and the outlines of some of the horses, but he couldn't see the approaching rider.

Then the moon was covered by a cloud. The rider had surely seen him, probably even while he was talking to the girl, but he had not called out. Not a good sign.

The Gunsmith kneeled behind the rain barrel, his Winchester at the ready, his eyes on the dim horse that was approaching around the side of the corral.

At first he thought there was no rider, that the saddle was empty. But now as the moon came from behind the cloud that had obscured the light, he saw that there was a rider, or something that could have been a rider, slumped in the saddle, leaning forward on the pommel, flopping a little as the horse came closer and nickered at Duke.

"Hold it," the Gunsmith called out. But he knew that whoever was in the saddle hadn't heard.

The horse had stopped now, only a few yards from where Clint was, but close to Duke, who shook his head, his bit jangling.

Carefully, Clint stepped out from behind the rain barrel. He crouched, waiting for a second or two, taking advantage of another cloud that had covered the moon. He took some quick steps toward the two horses, coming in on Duke's far side to protect himself from the rider whom he could make out slumped over the pommel of his saddle. He knew that whoever it was wouldn't shoot if he couldn't see him. At the same time, he knew the man was either seriously wounded or was faking it.

Once again the cloud moved away from the moon, and he could see the figure more clearly. No, the man wasn't faking it; of that he was sure. Yet, he took no chances, waiting for another cloud to shut out the light before he stepped forward and poked the barrel of the Winchester into the side of the slouched rider. Then he reached up his free hand and grabbed the man's shoulder. Suddenly the body moved, slipping out of the saddle and fell to the ground.

As Clint kneeled down the moon came out again. The rider was lying on his back, staring up at the deep, night sky. He was dead. And though the Gunsmith couldn't make out his face, he knew it had to be Cratcher.

He struck a lucifer and saw the blood. The whole head was a mess. The man's ears had been cut off.

The lean cowboy stepped back from the faro table, his right hand streaking for his six-gun, but his hand was suddenly seized from behind, and he winced as the gun barrel poked hard into his back.

But he was Texas and he was tough, and his tanned features darkened to an even deeper hue as he shouted to the faro dealer in his frustration, "You gaff devil! You be gaffing them cards!"

The dealer didn't even look up as two burly men detached themselves from the crowd which had formed about the cowboy. His arms were pinned to his sides and he was hustled to a rear door of the Hard Dollar Saloon and Gambling Hall. The click of poker chips, the purr of the wheels of fortune on the wall, the monotonous tones of the faro and monte dealers resumed after the brief intermission. In another moment it was as though nothing at all untoward had taken place.

Outside the rear of the Hard Dollar the stringy cowpoke picked himself up from the dirt street, slapped at his trouser legs and arms, and stamped his feet. He was swearing aloud when a man came walking toward him. The young drover hadn't seen him coming out of the saloon.

"What's the trouble, lad?" The voice was crisp, with a slight, unmistakable English accent. A medium-sized man, on the slender side, mustached, and with a strange air of graciousness about him.

The cowboy glared at him. "That dealer was using

a gaff hook on them cards. Son of a bitch ain't gonna be walkin' around long when I brace him again!"

"How much did you lose?"

"Twenty dollars."

Without a word, the man with the English accent handed the puncher a twenty-dollar gold piece. "That game wasn't crooked," he said. "But a man's betting against bad odds at any faro table. You should know that." He took a cigar out of his inside pocket, bit off the little bullet of tobacco at the end and lighted it.

The thick pillow of smoke almost hit the young cowboy in the face. The man's voice was now flecked with an unexpected hardness. "You got your money so don't come back here again."

Still disgruntled, the cowhand walked off muttering to himself.

Harry "Ace" DeWitt watched after him for a brief moment, then turned abruptly and walked back into the Hard Dollar.

Harry was born in England but came to Texas at age fourteen. When one day an older and bigger boy made the mistake of sneering at the smaller DeWitt boy, even calling him unsavory names, Harry ran all the way home, grabbed his father's shotgun and forthwith discharged a load of buckshot into the other boy's behind.

Luckily, the bully was not seriously hurt, but Harry was brought before the current justice of the peace and lectured roundly, then released.

He was twenty-five when he headed north out of Texas. When he hit Dodge he had eleven cents in his pockets; and while even then he was a shrewd one with the cards, 11 cents was not enough to allow entry into a game of poker. But he had a deck of cards, and he found an old barrel and rolled it down to where he found a busy street corner.

French monte was not a game considered for the established gambling halls, but most towns had a French monte artist or two operating with a polished barrel top in the street. All that was needed was a glib tongue and fast fingers.

Actually, French monte was simply a variation of the monte played in the gambling halls. Indeed, it was a new form of the old bunco artist shell game.

An ace and three other cards were dealt face up. They were then turned over so that only the backs showed. If the sucker could pick the ace, he was paid double his bet. Of course, this was impossible with any dealer who had any sort of claim to dexterity.

By the end of the first evening, Harry was thirty dollars ahead. Only a week later he had turned the thirty into three hundred, which was enough for a stake in a big poker game. At the end of the second week the DeWitt bankroll amounted to just a few dollars less than four thousand. He was on his way.

One or two more steps and Harry, now "Ace" joined forces with Sin Shavely, also a gambling man, and an entrepreneur of established reputation. Shavely was especially noted for two things: (1) his financial acumen, and (2) a tenacity in the pursuit of revenge that was awesome. Nobody—no one—ever double-crossed Sin Shavely and got away with it. And he looked the part—short, bent, older looking than he actually was, with eyes like gimlets, a slice for a mouth, and fingers that somebody once said resembled cant hooks. The perfect partner for Ace DeWitt.

Ace furnished the brains, the charm, the front, while Shavely carried the shovel, the rope, the lead pipe.

Together they opened the Hard Dollar in Prairie Falls and Junction. It was mostly under Ace's planning and direction. And of course, the dealers were honest. That is to say, honest in the eyes of the humble patron.

For instance, the young cowboy had been wrong about the Hard Dollar's faro dealer using a gaff, that small instrument shaped like a shoemaker's awl and attached to a finger ring, used by some dealers to pick whatever card from the faro box they wished. DeWitt and Shavely hoped—indeed, planned—to build the Hard Dollar into a very rich enterprise, and it would have been foolish to run crooked games. They of course knew very well that few of the big gambling houses did. They didn't have to. Like those bigger establishments, the Hard Dollar had set limits to bet on monte, faro, the wheels of fortune, and blackjack. There just was no chance for a player to double up on his bets.

But while Ace DeWitt was pleased to reap the rewards of his sharp endeavor—building his fortune, making good use of his partner's virtues in the field of land grants, the law, and shrewd influence amongst certain parties in the territorial capital—he did not start relaxing and looking forward to old age. He had bigger fish nibbling at his hook.

And he was therefore pleased one afternoon to see the man known as the Gunsmith pushing back the batwing doors of his establishment and walking in. It had been a while since DeWitt had had his talk with Clint Adams and he had almost wondered on his next move, since there had been no response from their initial meeting.

He had been standing at the far end of the bar, opening some bottles of wine—one of his most agreeable pastimes—and seeing who had entered, he nodded quickly to Clancy Fiddle, and turning, retreated into a back room.

As he closed the door behind him, his mind was racing. Clancy, of course would try to find out what Adams wanted. And of course, it could also be that he didn't want anything, other than a drink. Only then, why come to the Hard Dollar for his refreshment?

Clint had decided it was time to see DeWitt. It was clear that everything pointed to the gambler as the next step. As far as Wells Fargo was concerned, he was getting nowhere and had nothing to report to Cash Wilfong, other than his personal opinion, which was that whoever was running the road agents was no fool. Futhermore, in view of how Cratcher had received his comeuppance, it was clear somebody was playing for keeps. Had it been a friend of Kodl? Someone with a grim sense of humor, at any rate. Ears for those thumbs. Though Clint couldn't imagine a man such as Kodl—or Cratcher either—having friends.

When he'd first ridden into town and reported the killing to the local law—a gent named Warshower, wearing a marshal's badge and a Smith & Wesson in a well-worn holster—the news was received on the same level as tidings of the weather.

"Anybody plant him?" Warshower had asked,

peering casually at the Gunsmith from under thick gray eyebrows.

"Two of the passengers offered to, matter of fact," Clint said, "but the driver said he'd bring the body in on the stage."

"Where was yourself?"

"Rode in. I wasn't on the stage."

"That big black gelding, huh?" The marshal squinted at him. "Reckon I was out of town when you first rode in, but I heard you was here."

"I am here peaceful," the Gunsmith said. "I generally talk to the law when I come to a new town, but like you say, you weren't in your office."

"Who d'you think did it?"

"Shot, chopped up Cratcher? I don't know."

"Somebody what knowed about him taking Kodl's thumbs, I'd say."

Clint had let it go at that, and took his departure.

His next move had been in the direction of the woman named Melanie Lansing. He remembered her name now. The young girl at the stage depot looking for her sister had sparked his interest in the woman Ace DeWitt had wanted him to meet. Who could tell. There might be a lead somewhere. And he certainly wasn't making any headway as it was now.

He had approached the dragon planted behind the desk of the Junction House. The whey-faced proprietress—not only with the big desk between herself and the Gunsmith, but that enormous bosom as well—narrowed her little eyes to the point where they seemed to disappear. She was breathing heavily, and clearly had been dining on onions.

"Why you want to know? You got yer eye on that young tail?"

"I don't know the lady's age," Clint had said, bland.

"Hell, there ain't a one what's too old when you got a hard on. Ain't that the truth!" And her face seemed to split wide open as a roar of laughter burst from her. "Hell, Mr. Gunsmith, I told you I get a percentage for that kind of action." And suddenly her jovial humor had vanished to be replaced by a cold, hard glare, peering out of her fat rolls of cheek with the malevolence of a viper.

"I only asked you if the person was stopping here," Clint said patiently. "I don't even know her, or what she looks like. But a friend of mind mentioned her to me and said to look her up."

"She ain't here."

"Gone?"

"She moved out yesterday. While you was out of town. Mister, it's the early bird catches the worm."

"You know where she went?"

"I do not. And I wouldn't tell you anyways."

"Why the hell not?" Clint demanded, beginning to feel a bit heated at the smart aleck behind the desk.

"Policy of the house, sir." And she blinked at him rapidly, several times, and with an expression of what Clint assumed she must be thinking was coy.

Without another word he turned and walked back out to the street. Dammit, he hadn't wanted to open his business to the old dragon, but on the other hand, he had to get things moving somewhere. The old snake might have given out something useful. Except she hadn't.

He had just started down towards the livery when Carmela's roar at his back brought him to a full stop. The giant was standing on the front step of the Junction House. Her huge arm was raised above her bullet-shaped head. She was waving what looked like a piece of paper.

"Forgot to give you this, mister . . ." She started to say Gunsmith, but he cut her off fast.

"Adams," he snapped. "The name is Adams."

To his astonishment her face took on a whole new expression, and he could only define it as something possibly related to a smile.

"Yessir!" And she handed him a letter. "Tried to get it opened unbeknownst to you, but I couldn't. Somebody stuck it tightern' a bull's ass in fly time."

And roaring with laughter she turned and disappeared into her hotel. Clint couldn't help grinning after her. He didn't recognize the handwriting, but it was obviously a woman's, and there was a slight odor of perfume coming from the green envelope.

The message inside was brief. "Dear Mr. Adams: You don't know me, but I have been wanting to meet you, as I am engaged in writing a history of the West for a New York publishing concern. Might we get together? I am stopping at the Junction House, but will be away for a few nights, until Thursday when I shall come back into town. I do hope we can meet. Yours, Melanie Lansing."

Today was Thursday, but she evidently had not returned, not to her hotel at any rate. It was then he had decided it was time to run into Ace DeWitt again—casually. At this point there were just too many coincidences going on for him to avoid the question that kept prodding him. Why had Ace DeWitt confronted him with such a cock-and-bull story?

Chapter Seven

When Clint Adams walked into the Hard Dollar he
had seen Ace DeWitt down at the end of the long
mahogany bar, had watched him disappear towards
the back room. He was glad for the moment it would
give him time to talk to Clancy Fiddle who was busy
setting up fresh bottles behind the bar. For thus far he
had discovered nothing of any real use concerning the
holdups.

There was a different man behind the bar now, and
Clancy who doubled as swamper, was sweeping out.
Clint knew that he would have to go through Clancy
to make contact with DeWitt, and vice versa. DeWitt
would reach him through the bartender-swamper.
Sensible, especially when you didn't want everyone
to know your business.

He picked up a glass of beer now and carried it to
a table in the back of the room. Heads had turned, and
he knew that shortly tongues would begin to wag.

He'd only had one drink of beer from the heavy
mug when Clancy Fiddle approached.

"Figurin' on bein' about for a spell?" he asked,
leaning on his mop, and making it appear as though
he was casually passing the time of day.

The Gunsmith nodded. "Figure to."

"Mr. DeWitt might want to see you."

Clint realized that DeWitt had instructed Clancy to say exactly those words, and in that way.

"Tell him I want to see him," he replied with a tight and slightly dangerous smile.

Clancy pursed his lips at that, and covered his reaction by leaning forward and making a pretense of wiping the tabletop.

"I'll tell him," he muttered, his lips and eyes tight.

Clint lifted his mug of beer. "There's a couple of inches left in there. I'll be here till it gets empty. You got me?"

"Gotcha." Clancy dropped his head quickly in a nod that looked like his neck was hurting.

"What's the matter with you?" Clint asked severely. "You get your head caught in a keyhole?"

Clancy scowled. "Fought my way to the bottom of a bottle of trail whiskey last night. Got a head big enough to fit a hoss."

Clint watched him shuffling away. The next move was up to Ace DeWitt.

The Gunsmith waited.

The Billings House was known not only for the quality of its cuisine and wines, but also for its growing appreciation of the customer's need to be faced with a hefty bill. The hotel, which stood on raised ground on the proper side of the railroad tracks, had a good view not only of the town, but also of the long sweep of grass, running into the timber and on up to the mountains that framed the whole tableau. Travelers often had their breath taken by the astonishing view. But of course they were travelers from the East. The average westerner was used to such beauty, and even if he wasn't he would never have admitted that the scene was something special. Such an admission would have been wholly out of character.

Big Bob Glendenning seldom had time to admire anything, other than certain women and his own face and figure in the mirror. Tall, lanky, with guttered cheeks, wholly clean shaven, with rather large ears and a set of wide, hairy nostrils at the end of a long, boney nose, he was impressive. He was well over six feet, and in consequence found it necessary to look down on other people. He looked down on them anyway, regardless of his physical height.

At the moment Big Bob was looking down the cleavage of Melanie Lansing while running his forefinger along the shoulder strap that supported—for the moment anyway—her chemise. Melanie's bare, creamy shoulders reflected the light of a brace of gas jets plus the rays of a stand of half a dozen wax candles, while on a table beside them a bottle of Mumm's and a bottle of Crug's Private Cuvee waited to be opened.

Big Bob's breath had lost its quiet rhythm which he had been able to maintain during the evening, but now with his guest half undressed he was roused to the point of passion which he, and clearly the lady too, had been building ever since they had entered his hotel room.

His fingers tickling along her shoulder suddenly gripped her strap and broke it. He did the same on her other shoulder. Then with a quick move pulled down her chemise, and her two erect teats sprang into view. At that moment she reached down and rubbed the palm of her hand on his erection.

"I want you naked," he said, having trouble with his voice.

"That's the best way to do it," Melanie said, her voice wholly practical.

In seconds they were totally naked and he had lifted her and carried her to the bed. She was down on him now, taking his erect organ in her mouth, licking it, and sucking up and down, while her fingers squeezed his balls. He meanwhile had his legs wrapped around her neck and was reaching down to squeeze her teats with his hands.

"I want you to fuck me hard this time," she said. "And fuck me long!"

"I fully intend to, my dear." And to make sure she heard him, he jammed his cock up high and hard and wiggled it around while she spread her legs almost up to the top of the bed and whimpered with ecstacy.

"Oh my God, that's it. That's it. Give me! Give me that cock! Give . . . give . . . give . . . !" And then they were pumping, with him driving it in and up as far as it would go, faster and faster until they came in a united explosion, their loins pumping until eventually slowing down and finally stopping in mutual completion.

After some moment he sat up and walked to the nearest bottle of champagne.

"Two minds with the same thought," she said laughing as he poured. "Sir, you certainly know how to entertain a lady. Though, I know I shouldn't flatter you."

"Afraid I'll ask for a lowering of price, are you?" And he laughed, and returned to the bed carrying the two glasses, sparkling with the amber fluid.

"I'm planning to raise my price, my dear."

"Why?"

"I'll tell you later."

He sat down and handed her the glass. "Why later? Why not now?"

She giggled and reached over and held his limp cock.

"Because I've learned one very important thing over the years."

"And that is?"

"Always do business with a hard cock, never with a limp one."

Through the big mirror behind the Hard Dollar's long mahogany bar, the Gunsmith watched Clancy moving toward the rear of the building. He lifted his beer mug and took a swallow. In a few moments Clancy reappeared and moved in behind the bar and began waiting on customers. He did not look in Clint's direction, thereby signifying that Ace DeWitt would be on hand shortly.

Clint had just lifted his beer again when he saw the gambler approaching.

"Well, Adams, good to see you hale and hearty after your, uh . . . little trouble up by Drago."

"News, as I believe I've heard more than once, travels fast. Especially bad news." The Gunsmith's words fell between them dry as bones.

DeWitt managed a grin. "In my business it's

necessary to keep an ear or two on the ground. Sometimes that saves a whole lot of trouble."

"What can I do for you, DeWitt?"

"I was wondering what I could do for you," the gambler countered.

"Nothing." And the Gunsmith stood up.

"Give me a moment, Mr. Adams?"

DeWitt had lifted his head toward the Gunsmith, but when Clint looked down at him quickly, the gambler had turned his attention towards two men who had just pushed in through the batwing doors.

In a flash he had turned back to Clint, standing beside him. "Please sit down, sir." The smile was engaging, the gesture of his open hand as he offered Clint a seat, welcoming.

Clint reseated himself, keeping his eyes calmly on the other man. He had not missed the look exchanged between the gambler and the two rough-looking individuals who had walked into the saloon and were now standing at the bar. There had been just the slightest nod from the nearest one. And Clint noted how both were adequately armed, meaning they were no forty-a-month cowpokes. Then he realized they were the pair he'd roughed up at Meg Fiddle's Eatery.

DeWitt had pulled his chair closer to the table, adopting an easy, confiding tone. "Actually, I wanted to ask you if you'd happened to contact Melanie Lansing."

"Is there any reason why I should?"

The gambler pursed his lips, then smiled. "Just thought you might have taken me up on what we talked about last time."

"I thought you understood, DeWitt, I'm not interested in being written about."

The gambler smiled, sleek as a fox. "I was thinking rather that you would be interested in not being written about."

"And I'm for sure not interested in blackmail either," Clint snapped, just as Clancy Fiddle came into view.

DeWitt raised both his hands instantly, as though for a holdup. His smile was broad, apologetic, at the same time his eyes were loaded with concern. "Adams, believe me, that blackmail is a word that never is permitted in either my thought or my vocabulary. Sir, let me assure you of that. Please! I insist on being understood!" His long hand touched Clint's sleeve. His whole attitude was one of supplication. Meanwhile, Clancy waited at an appropriate distance until the scene was over. The man certainly had power was the thought that ran through Clint's mind. The power to corrupt, to inspire loyalty that bordered on stupidity. He knew the type.

But he knew too that something extra was happening—the two men at the bar, the approach of Clancy Fiddle, DeWitt's bringing up the subject of the woman writer. He settled back in his chair, though losing none of his alertness.

Suddenly DeWitt switched his attention to Clancy, bulleting him with his eyes. "What is it!"

The bartender-swamper handed him a piece of paper, then waited in silent fidelity while his employer opened it, glanced quickly at its contents and then slid it into his coat pocket. Then, without even a look at the waiting Clancy, he turned toward Clint Adams.

Clint was actually enjoying the scene, for he made a point of studying human behavior. And more often than not what he had learned paid off when the chips were down and the finger hit the trigger.

Clancy, quick to realize that he was dismissed, had moved in the direction of the bar. Clint watched him, noticing that he looked over at the two gun toughs who were together at one end of the group standing at the bar. Now one of them moved away, leaving his companion there, and worked his way across the room to a table, not very far from where Clint sat with DeWitt.

"A barroom is an interesting place, is it not, Adams?" DeWitt cocked an eyebrow in the direction of the Gunsmith.

"What do you want, DeWitt? I mean, right now!"

"I want you on my side. It's that simple."

"Not interested. And it's that simple," Clint said and he got to his feet. He was watching the man at the end of the bar, while also seeing his companion at the other side of the room, realizing once again the high value of the big mirror that was so often in back of the saloon bars.

As he turned and walked away he saw—again thanks to the mirror—that the gambler had moved his hand away from his chin which he had been holding, so that his palm lay flat out. It was clearly the sign meaning "no action." There was a tight smile on the Gunsmith's face as he walked through the swinging doors. He had been ready. It wouldn't have been easy. But he had been ready. And as he hit the boardwalk and started along the street, he was wondering what it could be that Ace DeWitt was so eager to protect. For he had come to the question of how much the gambler really wanted him working on his side, and how much his offer was simply a ruse to get him out of the way. More and more it began to look like the latter was DeWitt's primary aim. Did that mean that DeWitt knew he was working with Wells Fargo? And if so, how could he have known? Cash Wilfong had said that there was a leak in the company, that the road agents had inside information on the shipments. And so it could also be that somebody had tipped off somebody about himself, somebody could have seen him with Wilfong, even though they had exercised extreme care to avoid such an eventuality. And now, did that mean that DeWitt was connected with the bandits?

Deep in thought, he came within inches of bumping into someone coming down the street in the opposite direction, only avoiding the collision thanks to his unique sensitivity to his own atmosphere.

The near collision however carried its reward—at least for Clint Adams—in that, to his great surprise, the party in question happened to be the good-looking blonde he had spoken to on the train at the time of the robbery.

This time she was smiling, catching her breath, as they stood there in the middle of the boardwalk, while other pedestrians had to move around them.

"Mr. Adams, you're just the man I've been looking for! Did you by any chance receive my note? I'm Melanie Lansing."

• • •

His eyes had dropped to her hand as she lifted her cup of coffee, and she smiled at him over the rim of the cup, taking just a sip.

"It's good and hot."

"Heat will sure kill the taste of bad arbuckle," Clint said, grinning.

"Arbuckle?"

"That's coffee. Cowboy lingo."

They were sitting in the dining room of the Junction House, suffering the ministrations of Carmela herself, since the waiter, a youth named Hoag, had unaccountably taken the day off. Carmela took a goodly time explaining that to her sole customers of the moment. Both were glad to get rid of her.

"She is rather much," the girl said, with a sigh as the owner-proprietress of the Junction House finally left them.

"You said you wanted to see me," Clint said. He had delayed bringing up the subject for as long as he could. First of all he had no wish to talk about himself, and secondly, he simply enjoyed this attractive young woman's company. She was just damned good-looking.

"Yes, I did." She lifted her hand, looking at her fourth finger which showed a slight indentation obviously left by a ring. She moved the finger back and forth, then dropped her hand to her cup. "First, I want to say that you're very observant. I suppose you have to be in your business."

"My business is gunsmithing," Clint said. "I repair, rebuild, and clean guns."

"But you are the Gunsmith, aren't you? I do have

the right person!" And her mouth formed an "oh" of alarm.

"That is what I am sometimes known as," Clint said firmly. "But if it's that what you want to write about, I'm sorry, I can't help you. On the other hand, if you want to learn something about guns, I'd be willing to give you lessons. For a price," he added.

She leaned back, still holding the coffee cup on the table before her, and regarded him quizzically.

"You are an unusual man, Mr. Adams."

"Because I don't wish to be written about?"

"That, yes."

"And . . . ?"

She was looking down at her hand, with her face thoughtful. "I . . . I guess I don't know."

"Don't know what?" he pressed.

"I guess you've taken the wind out of my sails."

"That's the way it goes. No offense."

"May I ask you a question, Mr. Adams?"

"You can always ask, miss. I don't guarantee an answer."

She laughed at that, coloring a little.

"Can you tell me *any*thing about yourself? Or about gunfighting? You see . . ." She leaned forward on the table, looking down at her hands, as though trying to find what she wanted to say in the best way. "You see, I've put myself in a most unenviable position."

"You mean you've already agreed to get a story, you've promised something?"

"To my publisher, yes. I'm afraid I've been rather a fool."

"Sorry. I can't help you there, Miss Lansing." He

sat back in his chair, with the attitude of a man who has come to the end of a meeting, or at least has finished with a subject.

She continued to look down at her hands which were folded together on the checkered tablecloth. Clint simply waited. It was obvious that more was coming. And he had a notion of what it was going to be.

A long moment passed, and then she raised her eyes. Her face had changed; it wasn't as soft as it had been. And the Gunsmith knew he'd been right.

"I'm afraid you've put me in an embarrassing position."

"I hardly think so, Miss Lansing." Clint was looking at her steadily, and his voice was firm. "I think it's pretty clear that you've put yourself wherever it is that you find yourself."

"But don't you see, I have to write something about you. I can't let my editor down!"

"That's something you'll have to work out." Clint pushed back his chair. He was starting to get annoyed with the lady.

"May I just ask you one more question before you go away?"

He was standing now, his hand on the back of his chair, and was looking down at her. She was so damned good-looking!

"Go ahead."

"I have to write something. Will you read it over?"

"You mean, before you turn it in to your editor?"

She nodded. "I think it's only fair that we have that sort of arrangement."

"And if I disagree with what you've written?"

"Then you can advise me on how to proceed. I think that's a fair offer. I really don't know what else to say."

"I do. No!" He put his hat on and stood looking down at her.

She was all at once more composed, seeming to flower under his disapproval. Her voice was calm, cool, and she was obviously collected. "I do think you're being very unreasonable, Mr. Adams. And besides, I would like to see you again." And she stood up suddenly and stuck her tongue out at him, and with her back straight as a ramrod marched out of the dining room.

Clint wanted to burst out laughing, except that at the same time he was still angry at her effort to manipulate him. Was she really working with DeWitt, he suddenly wondered. For they both had implied and even voiced the same tactic of blackmail.

When he walked out into the lobby, Carmela stood vast as a butte behind the desk.

"You hear what happened?" she said, glaring maliciously at him, as though whatever had taken place was his fault.

"You smiled at somebody, Carmela?" he said, his good humor returning in the face of her impossible scowl.

"Very funny! Not so funny, Mr. Smart Aleck, is the Billings & Rockland was held up again—and in the same place. Moose River."

Chapter Eight

Bill McGovern, the conductor on the B & R had not liked being held up the first time. He hadn't like it any more the second time, when at 1:15 in the afternoon, he felt the .38 poking into his back. Meanwhile, other men swiftly boarded the train, and the locomotive came to a stop. Four men entered the cars and held their guns on the passengers, at the same time stripping them of any valuables. Two other men disconnected the express car and sent the engine a few hundred feet down the tracks. The next stop was blowing open the safe, and the acquisition of payrolls amounting to somewhere between twenty thousand and twenty-five thousand dollars.

Two of the gang, carrying the loot in grain sacks, headed down the tracks towards the horses while two others backed off, flinging a few shots into the windows of the carriages just to discourage pursuit. Then they too turned and ran in their high-heeled boots toward their horses. Within a couple of minutes the packhorse brought just for the purpose was loaded and they were all in the saddle.

Down the track, Conductor Bill McGovern stood unsteadily on his bandy legs and swore that those son

111

of a bitches would not pull it off a third time, though he realized it was a different gang.

On through the remaining afternoon the gang rode, approaching their destination by a roundabout trail. It was nearly dark when they reached the stone face that pointed the entrance to Wild Horse Canyon.

Part way up the canyon the gang had built themselves a perfect hideout. Ten miles from Prairie Falls & Junction, in the wildest part of the mountains, they had found a place where wind and water had hollowed out a cave in the cliff. This they had covered over with rocks and logs, and had built a crude corral of boulders that would also serve as a breastworks.

The men were tired, but they were exhilarated. The holdup had gone without a hitch. Now it was dark, but it was safe to build a fire and boil coffee and put down some grub. A bottle was passed, though their leader made sure that the privilege was not abused. Presently, after some desultory talk, the tired men turned in. As the camp quietened into silence, a sickle moon rose behind a looming rimrock.

The man who had led the raid on the Billings & Rockland sat some distance from the now dead fire. He was not tired. He was listening to the snoring of the men around him. He was thinking.

He knew that by now news of the holdup would have reached Junction and that the telegraph wires would be humming. The kid would catch the news of it, as well as the law. His thoughts dwelt on that scene, the kid receiving the news that he had pulled off a repeat, and without a hitch. The kid would know who had done it.

He lifted his head now and looked at the sky. God,

it was good. It was great. To be back. To be free; riding wherever the hell he wished. He was damned if he was going to lessen his life, by God, for anyone or anything. Not for any goddam law! He never had—excepting that one time—and he never would again.

He grinned into the night, relishing the surprise he had brought. The astonishment! Well, by damn, he hadn't done all that bad with such a pickup bunch. It had been kind of a rush, but the time element had been a definite part of the agreement. He'd sure kept his end of the bargain. What was more, the haul was a good one. And the kid would know who had done it. He was sure of that. There would have been the surprise, finding someone had pulled off the train first. Then the anger. The kid would have been really burned. He'd had the news of the planned holdup from Deaf Charlie Banks, and so he'd stolen the march. He chuckled. Stolen the march. Hah! And stolen the big payroll,—not only from the railroad and Wells Fargo, but from the kid.

He was feeling suddenly tired. Not much, but enough to make him want to close his eyes. But just then as he nodded he heard the pebble, like a small tinkling.

Good enough. He'd picked good outriders. He was on his feet with the .38 in his fist when the figure formed out of the side of the bullberry bushes near where he had been sitting.

"Hello, kid," he said soft.

"Hello, Miller."

"I see you picked up on my message."

"I figure by now half the county has," Carisa Bolero said as she came closer to Miller Rhodes.

* * *

By now, Clint Adams had the report on the second holdup of the B & R train. Cash Wilfong had wired Marshal Honus Warshower that he had an ally in the person of Clint Adams. And he had wired a similar message to Clint.

The two men were sitting now in Warshower's office, on Main Street in Prairie Falls & Junction. There were just two chairs in the office, sufficient for their meeting. A potbellied, jumbo stove stood in the middle of the room, and though there was no need for it as far as the weather was concerned, it being early July, the marshal had built a fire and boiled up some coffee that—as Marshal Warshower put it—"could stand on its own feet." Since the brew smelled like tar and tasted likewise, the Gunsmith could do no more than agree with him.

"So you got a good bit of recovering to do," Warshower was saying. "I'll throw in with you, but I ain't got any deputies. Had a couple last year but they run off to join the road agents. the sons of bitches."

"This woman? They joined the woman who held up the B & R last time? Or was it somebody else?"

"I dunno."

It was the day after the second holdup, and as luck developed, a heavy rain had wiped out all possibility of pursuit. Warshower had hit the trail—what little there was of it—with two pickup deputies, who, in his own words, "wasn't worth a pisspot between 'em" and had only just returned. He was tired, angry, and totally thwarted.

"Sons of bitches got away with nigh to twenty-five thousand dollars. And then by God it has got to rain.

It ain't rained a drop for a week, but it has to rain this time right now. Shit! I mean shit!" He reached furiously into the pocket of his shirt and pulled out a cold cigar stub. Then, taking out a wooden match he struck it one handed on his thumb nail. In another moment his head was half obliterated in a cloud of blue, foul-smelling smoke.

"The passengers," Clint said. "You talked to some of the passengers?"

"And the engineer and fireman, and Bill McGovern. Nobody killed, like I told you already, but McGovern, the poor bastard, got a gun barrel crost the side of his thick Irish head. Poor bastard. Nobody else hurt though."

"But none of the passengers were molested?" Clint was leaning forward with all his attention, trying to picture the holdup. "Did anybody spot their horses?"

"Somebody said he saw a buckskin. Someone else said he saw a bay horse with a white blaze and stockings."

"Easy enough to paint those markings," Clint said. "Though the buckskin might be a lead. How did they behave, the men? I mean, were they in a hurry? Did anybody speak. Or did they use sign language, or a whistle?"

"Both," Warshower said, warming up as his interest in the details the Gunsmith was asking for took over from his annoyance. "Same as our friend Carisa. No bullying, no making everybody hurry up. All neat and clean as apple pie."

"Then how come you think it wasn't Carisa? It sure sounds like her."

Warshower wagged his head, scratched into his

beard. "Dunno. But, there was similar doings. I mean, nobody saw the leader, that they'd know him as such."

"You're saying that there was no one person giving orders."

The lawman nodded. "It could of bin Carisa, you know. But I just got a hunch it wasn't."

"Why?"

"Well, I got something from Bill, from McGovern. See, Bill was real mad about being held up that last time. And 'course, we don't know that was Carisa either. We was just supposin' it could of bin her. But this time, Bill, he had stowed a Greener .12 gauge in the signal box behind the smoker section. He went for it, and that was when the big son of a bitch hit him alongside his head. Poor bastard was lucky he didn't get shot."

"But that sounds like the woman's tactics to me, not shooting. Remember, last time, the holdup I saw, McGovern was also hit. I recollect that big welt he had on the side of his head."

Warshower shrugged. "Well, I dunno. I could be dead wrong, but I don't believe it was Carisa Bolero and that little son of a bitch husband of hers."

But Clint was still puzzled. "Let's look at it," he said slowly, putting down his mug of unfinished coffee. "The first train holdup went smoothly. Nobody got hurt, except McGovern, who being Irish was likely spoiling for a fight against injustice and wouldn't take it lying down."

"He is a scrappy little bugger. Tough as nails," the marshal put in.

"Then the stage holdup with Cratcher getting his

ears cut off. Though we know Carisa ran that one, we don't know that she had anything to do with Cratcher."

"But she did beat up on her friend Tiny Blue."

"But that was on her husband. It wasn't on one of the passengers."

"This time with the second train holdup still nobody was hurt, except McGovern. Yet you tell me you believe it wasn't Carisa."

"I dunno why. Maybe I'm crazy. And I wouldn't want to put my hand on the good book."

"There is something here we're not seeing," Clint said. "Something staring right at us. You know what I mean?"

Warshower nodded. "Then for one thing, 'course at the train holdup nobody spotted anyone that even could of bin Carisa. Like you saw somebody small, slender. It don't mean it was her."

"It doesn't mean it wasn't her, either," Clint said. "Don't forget, she was very much seen at Drago Gulch Depot." And then, looking carefully at War-shower he said, "I recollect hearing she used to hang out with Miller Rhodes."

"That she did."

"But he disappeared—maybe a couple of years back. That right?"

"That is right. Excepting, it was more like five, six years. Anyhow, nobody knows what happened to Miller. Some say he was shot up on his last job, and some say he was taken and sent to Folsom, but I don't have any record of that. Then there's the story he hit for South America. That's the one sounds most likely to-meself." He blew out a big cloud of smoke from his stogie and then fell into a fit of coughing.

"Carisa used to be in his gang, that right?"

"He met her when she was a kid, long way back. So I've heard anyways. And he taught her. Let me tell you, that young woman is smart as a firecracker on the Fourth of July. And she is tough."

Clint Adam's was looking tightly at the marshal.

"I see you got something on your mind," War-shower said.

"Would you say those two were really close?"

"She was his woman."

"That is what I have heard. But I mean, maybe even more than that. You say he met her when she was a kid. You mean, really young? Ten, eleven?"

"I dunno. I'd figure maybe fifteen, somewhere like that."

"What I'm getting at is that she could have been really attached to him, more than say someone she'd meet when she was older. You follow my drift?"

The lawman nodded, billowing out more smoke, and this time it was the Gunsmith who was hit by a coughing attack. The marshal of Prairie Falls and Junction didn't appear to notice.

"Holy Moses," said Clint, his eyes watering. "That thing would bring a bull buffalo to his knees."

"It tastes real good."

"Glad to hear it. Now, getting back . . . would you allow that some road agents, like some gunmen, have what you might call a way of doing things? Like . . . a style."

"Why, I do believe so. If you mean, you can

sometimes tell by the way a job was handled who done it."

Clint was nodding, his eyes, face, his whole body concentrated on the thought he was following.

"Maybe Carisa picked up Miller's style."

"I wouldn't say no to that. But what does that get us?"

"It gets us to the question of maybe Mr. Miller Rhodes is back."

Honus Warshower, marshal of Prairie Falls and Junction opened his mouth in big surprise and his cigar fell out. This caused him to grab the stogie from his belly before his clothes caught on fire. In the action, he knocked over his mug of coffee and in standing, kicked back his chair so that it hit the wall with a clatter.

"Jesus!" He glared at the Gunsmith who was grinning at him. "Jesus Christ!"

When Clint returned to the Junction House, Carmela pushed a note toward him across the top of the desk.

"Maybe you hit gold after all," she said, her little eyes gleaming at the thought of gossip.

"Strictly business," Clint replied, deciding now to just go along with her.

"Glad to see you're a man gets around."

"So am I." Without looking at the note he put it in his shirt pocket and started up the stairs.

"Ain't 'cha gonna read it" Carmela demanded, glaring up at his retreating figure.

"I know what it says," Clint called back over his shoulder.

"Hah! so do I, you smart-ass buzzard," muffling the last words, so that he barely heard them. At any rate, he caught their gist.

Clint Adams continued up the staircase, with the appalling feeling suddenly appearing in him that he really didn't dislike the owner-manager of the Junction House, as a matter of fact. But he refused to let the thought grow further.

When he got to his room and opened the note he discovered that he was right about its contents. Yes, it was from Melanie Lansing, and yes she wanted to talk with him, but her suggestion for a meeting was interesting. Would he be interested in a horseback ride and a picnic. She would be back in the Junction House around noon if he wished to contact her.

He lay down on his bed. There was a good hour till noon, and he decided this was a moment to try and piece things together. So many loose ends made it difficult to know how to proceed. Yet, he felt the need to keep in contact with Lansing. If only for the reason that DeWitt had tried to manipulate him into that connection. And so there was obviously more there.

And yet, at the same time, what did Lansing and DeWitt have to do with the road agents? Maybe nothing. But if nothing, then why had DeWitt approached him, and why had the girl? In both cases it had come from them. Maybe they were working together? Anyway, why would either of them try to tout him off his interest in the Wells Fargo shipments?

He sat up and lighted a quirly. Obviously, he needed more material to work with. All to the good then that he see Melanie Lansing. Not to overlook the fact that she was obviously built for sex. She had it coming out of her pores, as far as he could tell. And it would be simply criminal if he didn't investigate the possibilities that were so clearly evident.

He had just decided to put out his smoke when he heard the step in the corridor outside, and then saw the slip of white paper being pushed under the door.

"I am back. I await your decision with baited breath!!! Melanie"

He was grinning as he stubbed out his quirly. The lady was fun.

While he kept an office in Billings and a room in Junction, Big Bob Glendenning made his main headquarters in San Francisco, where he had built a mansion and where he kept his wife, with whose fortune he had started out in his life of commerce, and where his children had grown up. Big Bob was famous as a strong family man. This colorful description fooled no one, least of all his wife, and certainly not his incredibly numerous amours. Yet, he was good to his family. He didn't disgrace them, and in their own way he knew they were fond of him.

Using his wife's money, he had built his powerful stage line, and it had prospered even beyond his own high dreams. He was well satisfied for a decent length of time. He attended to business, bought a ranch, enjoyed his life. Until two things happened: (1) the Billings & Rockland began to run track into stage line territory, and (2) he met Melanie Lansing and fell in love with her. He began losing money on his stage lines, for the railroads were taking business right and left; and he began spending large sums on "the love of my life." The lady, it turned out, was more than delighted to receive his financial attentions, and her demands for the various niceties she required, including hard cash, began to grow.

But the stagecoach king, as he was sometimes called, had one other weakness besides women. He was a shrewd businessman—hadn't he built the "toughest stage line in the West"?—but he loved to gamble, and here he was not always shrewd. Every man, he told himself, had some one weakness; even the greatest men had a "divine failing." It was only a matter of time when he found he owed money to Harry DeWitt. It was only a matter of a little more time until Mr. DeWitt sympathetically offered him a solution.

All over the West the stage lines were giving way to the railroads. Even Wells Fargo itself was endangered, or so it seemed. Big Ben Holladay had gone down and so had Butterfield. Indeed, Wells Fargo was the last of the really giant companies still in operation. While the Glendenning coaches were being rented to them on certain lines, there was still some income. But lately, especially around the goldfields, the stages were taking a beating, and now even the trains were being hit more and more. Big Bob was on the point of putting his San Francisco mansion on the market when Harry DeWitt had made an offer.

It was simple. Dump the stageline and get into the railroads. Clearly there was soon going to be track ribboning the whole of the American continent.

Glendenning had told Ace DeWitt that he didn't know he was a railroad man.

"I'm a gambler," DeWitt had said. "I bet on how many drinks a man'll take before falling down."

"And you're betting on the railroads. I think you're right. You've convinced me."

"You go along with me," DeWitt had said, "and we'll forget about that little matter of poker money."

"What do you want—specifically?" Big Bob had asked.

"Simple," the gambler had said. "I want you to get rid of your stage line."

"Sell it? To whom?"

"You can't sell it. There's no one to buy it."

"Then how?"

"I want you to wreck it."

"I don't understand," Big Bob had said, feeling alarm striking through him. "How can I wreck my own stage line?"

"You don't have to do a thing. Just let the road agents take it."

"That sounds crazy, DeWitt."

"Nobody's going to buy your line. You could just stop it, but the risk would be that somebody else might start up another line. If the bandits take it over, I mean, by scaring the hell out of everybody and showing Wells Fargo, for example, that it doesn't pay to ship by stage . . ." He had held his hands open, as though the explanation was that clear and therefore unnecessary. "I want people to be afraid to travel by stage. You get it now?"

It had hit Bib Bob like a blow in the guts. But he had gotten it. And after a struggle he had accepted it, plus the financial arrangement. But he was not happy. He was not happy at all when he heard from DeWitt that a man known as the Gunsmith was in town, probably on behalf of Wells Fargo.

• • •

Clint Adams felt the hot sun on his bare back as he lay on top of the girl, spent, and suffused with the peaceful joy that came after a full bout of lovemaking. He was still inside her, and as he shifted his weight a little she murmured in his ear.

"It's wonderful."

"That is what it's supposed to be," he said, withdrawing from her, while her fingers clutched at him, reluctant to let him go. But she didn't insist, and he rolled off her, and lay on his back, with his arm pillowing her head.

"God, it smells so good," she said, her voice still drowsy.

The sun was hot on his chest and belly now, and on his crotch and legs too.

"I knew you'd be good," she said.

"Yeah. I knew it too," said the Gunsmith.

"You conceited beast." But there was laughter in her words. She lifted herself up onto her forearms and elbow and looked down at him, her blond hair spilling down onto her shoulder and her big, tight, hanging breasts. Leaning down she tickled one nipple across his lips, until he opened his mouth and began to suck.

The nipple was hard and large, supported by a firm teat that she was now pushing into his mouth, his whole face. With his other hand he was squeezing its companion, while she, for her part, had reached down and was stroking his rigid organ that was already sleek with come. In the next moment she rolled up and onto him and sat down right onto his big peg, straddling him with her thighs and sinking his shaft deep and high inside her. As he continued to suck and play with both her teats, alternating now, from one to the other, and even trying in vain to get both of them into his mouth at the same time.

In another moment she withdrew and went down on him, taking the entire length of his shaft into her mouth, down her throat. While he slid his middle finger into her soaking bush and lips and wiggled it and stroked, while she began to gasp and at last released his organ while he brought her down on her back and mounted her in the orthodox fashion.

Now began the long, sinuous movement of their loins, as he rode her deliciously and she stayed right with him, not missing a stroke.

Slowly, then changing his pace, he stroked her towards the climax, but then nearly there, he almost drew out, not completely, only to the ridge just below the head of his organ. And then he began the slow thrusting which would work them both slowly into their next stage, which would be a faster movement, until finally they were thrashing each other, their bodies entwined as one . . . faster and faster, and deeper and higher until it became absolutely impossible, and together they exploded in a shattering, exquisite release of all that had built up within them . . . every last delicious drop.

Later, as he half dozed beside her, he suddenly remembered the girl at the stage depot at Drago Gulch; the blond who'd said she was traveling to Prairie Falls to look up her sister, Melanie Lansing. He had forgotten about her, yet now carried the memory of a rather sweet smile, sad blue eyes, and a very—indeed very—fine figure, besides a bosom that just bordered on being outrageous. Idly now, he wondered if the girl had contacted Melanie. He thought of mentioning the incident, the girl, but decided no. There was something missing, or not right. Caution, at any rate, good sense, stayed him; and he decided to wait and do nothing. If the girl Melanie brought up the subject, then he could respond with his information. It was just that somehow he felt something wasn't quite right.

"What are you thinking about?" his companion suddenly asked, as she snuggled even closer to him.

"I was thinking that I was feeling a little hungry, and wondering what you might have there in the way of the picnic you mentioned in your note."

"Do you want to know what I was thinking about?" she said softly.

"What?"

"I was thinking how much I wanted to make love with you—I mean, 'right now' as those staunch westerners say!"

"Funny."

"What?"

"I was thinking the same thing. I mean, like those fancy-pants dudes like to say."

"And so are you ready?" she said, reaching over to his belly, and running her fingers downward.

"Why I reckon I am ready, ma'am; good an' ready I mean right now to lock horns with that there purty little lady!"

Big Bob Glendenning, as everybody knew, had an eye for a pretty girl. He was proud of that fact. His raunchy friend Melanie had commented, not unfavorably, on this characteristic of his. She had also commented colorfully at one point that at his age he should try to lay off using his erection "like a dowsing rod." Her remark had amused him greatly.

Big Bob was thinking of Melanie as he walked down the main street of Prairie Falls on a bright afternoon and all at once spotted the young blonde with the sad blue eyes coming towards him. The girl looked familiar. Did he know her? He was sure not, for he wouldn't forget such a pretty face and fine figure as that.

In the next moment she looked at him, and caught him staring at her. Coloring, she looked away and started to hurry by with her head down.

But at that point something happened. Somebody jostled him—or was it her?—and he stepped away, moving quite unintentionally into the girl. The boardwalk was crowded and he even struck another person.

"Excuse me!" His words burst from him, with a ring of delight for the excuse that had happened so naturally.

"That's quite all right, sir." Her voice was soft, and he realized she was younger than he had thought.

"Very clumsy of me."

"It's crowded." And she made as if to go by him, but he was blocking her path.

"My name's Bob Glendenning," he announced, doffing his big hat. "I believe you must be a stranger in town and I deeply regret lack of courtesy on my part."

She said nothing to that, but as she turned her head he remembered that he had seen her in the stage office down the street following the holdup at Drago Gulch.

"Ah! I was trying to remember where I'd seen you

before. I was staring at you as you came down the street—do forgive me—because I knew I'd seen you. And now I do remember. It was at the stage depot, following your very unpleasant experience at Drago Gulch."

She was staring at him with an expression of astonishment on her pretty face, which he found marvelous.

"Yes." he went on. "You see I felt responsible for your inconvenience at the hands of those bandits, for I try to insist on the comfort of each and every one of my passengers."

"I do believe I remember seeing you, sir, but I was so upset . . ."

"Look, let me, do allow me to take you to dinner. I mean, to make up at least in small part for your harrowing experience."

Not waiting for her reply, he took her arm and escorted her towards the Junction House dining room.

It was past noon, and the room was almost empty. He was glad for that. He picked a table in the corner and without further ado ordered a bottle of wine.

"Do tell me your name," he said when the waiter had left them. "I've already told you mine. Bob Glendenning."

"I remember it," she said, suddenly laughing. "I'm Miriam Landusky."

"Where are you from?"

"St. Mary's, in Ohio."

He felt something clutch at him then. He remembered Melanie telling him she came from a town called St. Mary's. But he held his tongue.

As they proceeded through the meal, accompanied

by a fine white wine, he learned more of her, not only to his pleasure as she opened to him, but to his great surprise.

"I'm looking for my sister, Melanie. Melanie Lansing." Her blue eyes were large and liquid as she looked at him. "Would you know her, sir?"

Glendenning dropped his fork on the floor and bent down to pick it up. The ruse worked, and for the moment he was able to get away without answering her. Instead, he came out with a question.

"How long is it since you've seen your sister? And is she expecting you?"

"It's been some years, and no, she isn't expecting me. You see, I've sort of tracked her down. Our . . . mother passed away. Dad died while Melanie was still at home. That was when she left. The last I heard she was working for some newspaper in Chicago. But she's not expecting me. I'm afraid she might not even recognize me."

"Would you recognize her?" Glendenning asked.

"The day I got here I thought I might have seen her, but then, whoever it was, was gone in the crowd. And I didn't follow."

Glendenning's face showed his surprise. "But you didn't speak to her? You didn't follow her?"

"I . . . I guess I wasn't sure. You see, I don't know whether she would want to . . ." Suddenly her eyes filled with tears and she bowed her head and began looking for her handkerchief.

Big Bob was swift with his. "Permit me, my dear, uh, Miriam."

"You see, when Melanie left home, she was very angry, and upset. I don't want to go into it. But she did write, and then it was all right. I had letters from her, and I wrote her. But then suddenly the letters stopped, a long while back. And when Mother died, well then I decided to try to find her. I got a lead at the newspaper."

"What an adventure," Glendenning murmured sympathetically. "You must have suffered, my dear. By the way, where are you stopping?"

"At a place, a rooming house, run by a Mrs. Thorpe."

Glendenning leaned carefully forward, torn between his admiration for the girl's looks and his concern whether or not to admit that he knew Melanie. Yes, they did look alike, and he even felt now that the girl in front of him was the prettier, the more attractive, and yes, the more seductive! The seductiveness of innocence, of course.

"And who else knows of your search for your sister, Miriam? I mean, who in Prairie Falls?"

"Only one person, and I've not been able to locate him."

"And who is that?" Big Bob asked picking up his glass of wine.

"His name is Clint Adams. But I don't know; perhaps he has already gone on somewhere. I don't believe he was from these parts."

Big Bob Glendenning very nearly dropped his glass of wine.

"Do you think you could help me, Mr. Glendenning?"

He didn't answer immediately. Inside he was cursing the coincidence, the luck that had brought that damned Gunsmith to Prairie Falls. And even now with this girl, the man had to be in on it in some way. Damn him! Damn him!

Then he cleared his throat and said, "I will try to help you, my dear. I'll do some asking around. As a matter of fact—now I don't want to get your hopes up—but, well, I might know your sister, or maybe know someone who knows her."

She was sitting bolt upright in her chair, and all at once. "Do you meant that? Golly, that would be so great!"

"I can't promise anything."

"But have you seen her, spoken with her, or is it that you know someone who might know Melanie. Oh, I wish you could help me!"

"You see, it's that often people coming out west change their name for some reason or other. And so one cannot be sure. But I promise you, I'll do my best. Meanwhile, I advise you strongly—and I must place this condition to any help I might render you—that you must not talk to anyone about this situation. Tell nobody!"

"But why? Why not tell anybody? How am I going to find Melanie if I can't ask about her."

His voice was tinged with authority now as he looked steadily at her. "My dear Miriam. I have said that I will help you. I pledge my full support. But you know, sometimes there are reasons why people come out west, change their names, and don't communicate with their families. This is not to suggest that Melanie has done anything she'd be ashamed of. You understand? One has to go carefully. For, after all, you wouldn't want to hurt your sister in some way out of ignorance of her position. It's obvious that she must have started a new life. Do you understand?"

There were tears on her cheeks. He thought she looked adorable. "Oh, I do understand. And I'm sorry. It's just that I've been looking so forward to seeing Melanie. We were so close when we were younger. I can't tell you how I've missed her."

"I understand," Big Bob Glendenning said gravely.

"And I want you to know I understand what you're saying, too. Especially about not talking to anyone."

"Not to anyone," he said. "Not to that man you met. What was his name? I can't remember."

"Adams. Clint Adams."

He smiled at her now, watching the tears dry on her cheeks as her eyes lighted up with the anticipation of finding her sister.

"I will keep in close touch with you, my dear. We will work together on this. I can't promise you anything, except my unquestionable loyalty and my strong effort." He reached over and took her hand which was lying on the table. For an instant he felt her fingers stiffen, but then they let go, and she let him hold her.

He felt the thrill moving through him now like fire. By damn! She was even better looking than Melanie. And from what he could imagine through her well-filled dress, her body had to be equally as good if not better. Moreover, she was younger. And in his summation, youth was a major factor. Young. God, he could teach her!

Big Bob was beaming with anticipation as he walked Miriam Landusky down to Mrs. Thorpe's rooming house and left her.

Chapter Nine

In the moonlight falling in the camp at Wild Horse Canyon the shapes of the sleeping men were barely visible. A horse nickered, but for no apparent reason. There was the sound of snoring from a few of the prone bandits.

A short distance away from the sleeping figures, the dead campfire, the man and the woman sat by the soft glow of a second fire. They sat together in quiet conversation, interspersed with silences, while behind them a single bedroll lay in total disarray from their lovemaking.

"It's been a long time," Carisa said again.

He turned his head toward her slightly, just enough to cut his eye. "You got a man, huh, Kid?"

"I've got a husband."

"Get rid of him."

"I already did."

"That little son of a bitch?"

"How'd you figure?"

Miller Rhodes didn't answer that question. Instead he said, "Can you trust him?"

"No."

He grinned. "Good girl. I see you learned your lessons."

"I had a good teacher," Carisa said, slipping her hand along his thigh.

He put his hand over hers.

"Miller . . ."

"Huh . . . ?"

"How's it been?"

"I was down in New Mex, did some cowpunching, but mostly breaking hosses. But the Pinkertons were also after me, plus Wells Fargo."

"Any of the boys with you?"

"Now and again. Had to move about. But you know how I like cowboyin', especially busting broncs."

"I know you got the reputation for it."

He released her hand, scratched at his back. She gave a little laugh and reached over and scratched him, hard.

"It's been a while since I done that to you."

"A little to the left; more. That's the spot."

"Around here they think you're in the pen or sweet dead."

"That is what I know. And we'll keep it that way."

"I had a notion you were in the country," she said. And her dark eyes were shining.

"I had a notion you were about, too. The way you pulled that train job."

She gave a little laugh of pleasure. "That was my first train. And when you pulled the next one at the same spot I knew for sure you were in the country. Why'd you wait so long?"

"Kid, you still got things to learn. Living the way people like us do is one of the things. There is still bounty on me."

"Men hunting you. Marshals and . . ."

"All kinds. You want to join the pack?"

"Miller, that ain't funny."

"Cratcher found out it wasn't so funny. The son of a bitch."

"You? Did you, you cut him?"

"No. That was Beems. He was riding with me. Beems was a pal of Kodl, and Cratcher cut off Kodl's thumbs."

"Is Beems gonna be with us?"

"No."

"What do you think they'll do now?"

"The law?"

"Uh-huh."

"I dunno. I speak to them as little as possible."

They both had a laugh at that.

"Miller . . ."

"Speaking of Cratcher, you screwed up at the stage depot. You fucked the whole thing."

"Miller . . ."

"Acted like you forgot every damn thing I ever taught you! Acted like a goddamn greener with a stake up her ass!"

"But I—"

"But I nothing! All on account of that little son of a bitch. I heard it all."

"From who!"

"Don't matter. How you acted so fuckin' jealous. You damn fool, don't you remember how many times I told you not to allow personal anything when you're on a job! Shit!"

"Miller—"

"Shut up . . ." He held up his hand, then reached

with his other for the scattergun on the ground beside him.

"Somebody?"

"You getting deef beside everything else?"

In the dark she flushed with shame. She hated it when she made mistakes. Yet, later she always appreciated his pointing things out, as he sure didn't hesitate to do. He had taught her, and he knew his stuff back and forward and all around the barn.

She had reached for her six-gun now, loosening it in its holster.

"Could be the boys," Miller said then. And he stood up, and moved quickly and silently towards the protection of the trees that ringed the clearing. She followed, keeping a good distance between them, as he had taught her.

When they were almost at the stand of spruce he signaled with his hand, and she moved off to the left, entering the timber about fifty yards away from him. An enemy approaching over the open area would be in cross fire.

Good enough, he reflected, as he saw where she entered the timber. She was still on the point, at least most of the time, and by God she was still his woman.

In the late afternoon the town seemed to take a moment to doze, as though the ticking heat had something to say before leaving the land. It was a moment that Clint Adams always honored. The day was done, and now it was the time for night. As he crossed Main Street after leaving Clint Fiddle's livery, he saw Clinch Fiddle sitting outside his carpenter shop and undertaking establishment.

Clinch appeared to be the oldest of the Fiddle boys, looking some sixty going on seventy. He was chewing thoughtfully, spitting now and again as he leaned back in his beaten-up wooden chair, tilting back on two legs. He watched the man known as the Gunsmith walking along the boardwalk and finally entering the marshal's office. Then, looking back down towards brother Clint's livery, he saw the riders, Mike Wagner and Ollie Kitchner from the the Crossbones outfit.

He didn't move, just took it in as the pair approached along the street. He knew them, their type—swift mouths and guns. He wondered if they'd been following the one known as the Gunsmith. It didn't seem so now, as they turned off the boardwalk to enter the Moosehead.

He had heard from Meg Fiddle about the boiling water in her café. How Adams—whatever his name was—had thrown the water on the one and hit the other with the heavy pot. A good man. Well, his sister-in-law could take care of herself. He knew that. But now the thought that was under all that, the thought lying in the back of his mind came again to the surface. It concerned the body in his icehouse out back. The body of Cratcher.

For some reason he kept thinking of Cratcher. Cratcher with his ears cut off. What a mess! And he minded the time Cratcher had cut off Kodl's thumbs. That was the least of it. The most of it was Cratcher torturing that poor son of a bitch, though for sure Kodl was a real son of a bitch. As was Cratcher, by God. Neither one a choir boy!

Well, he was waiting for word from Bob Glendenning on what to do with Cratcher. Why they hadn't let him just bury him right now he didn't understand. But word had come that Glendenning was going to pay for him anyway, but wanted him to wait a day or two. Meanwhile, Cratcher was on ice. He would like to get rid of him. He'd handled plenty of bodies in his time, but this one gave him a funny feeling. He'd handled all kinds of corpses, shot, cut, beaten, and the regular kind, too. But Cratcher. He scratched his head. He would just sure like to get rid of him.

Now the sun was just reaching the roof of the livery barn and Clinch figured it was time for a glass of something or other. He had just stood up, stretched and had run both gnarled hands inside his yellow galluses when he saw the man they called the Gunsmith coming out of Honus Warshower's office.

The thought flashed through his mind that it must have been a quick visit when he saw Wagner, minus his partner from the Crossbones coming out of the Moosehead. And he knew something was wrong. On account of you just about never saw one of that pair without the other. But Clinch had no time to give that surprise any thought, for Mike Wagner had walked right into the middle of the street and stood there, looking at the Gunsmith feller. He stood there, and by golly you could see he was ready.

"Hey, Gunsmith! I'm gonna even it now, you son of a bitch!"

Clinch's jaw must have dropped then—at least that was how he later figured his chew fell out of his mouth—for he saw Wagner slapping leather, and at the same time he knew why he hadn't seen Kitchner. But then he wasn't sure what he saw happen, until he pieced it all together later with the help of a couple of other witnesses.

Wagner went for his iron, but the Gunsmith man seemed to ignore him, for he'd already turned, drawn his own six-gun and shot Ollie Kitchner real dead. Ollie tumbled right off that roof of Herb Morrisson's General Store, and before he hit the street that Mister Gunsmith had drilled Mike Wagner right between the eyes. Mike died with his unfired six-gun clenched in his fist.

It was a few moments after that when Clinch realized he'd dropped his chew without even knowing it. As he stood there in front of his carpenter's shop and undertaking establishment, he realized that Cratcher was going to have company that night in the icehouse. He couldn't have said why, but somehow he felt better for that.

"Did you see it?" Clint asked Warshower.

"I think you need two people to watch you, Adams; you're that fast."

"What I meant was, did you see it was self-defense?"

"Those two have been long overdue," the marshal of Junction and Prairie Falls said as they returned to his office for another cup of coffee. "But somebody set that up. That wasn't only their idea, even though you did whipsaw them at Meg's place."

"That's what it looks like to me," Clint said.

"Got any ideas who?"

Clint shook his head.

Warshower looked at him gravely. " 'Pears to me like somebody don't like you."

"I sure would never have guessed that," Clint said, dry as a mustard plaster.

The marshal gave a wry chuckle. "What I am saying is that whoever set that up is likely to try again. You know 'course, you're a target no matter where you go."

"I'm beginning to get that notion," the Gunsmith said drily.

"You been pressing on these holdups. I got my ears around town. And that's what I hear. Like, I know you. I know why you're here. But I know you been damn careful the way you get your information, if you've even been able to get any. What I'm saying is that you ain't left any trail of smoke back of you. You've been clever, smart. That means somebody knowed about you maybe even before you come here. That's what I'm getting at."

"I can't argue with that. I'd lay odds on it that someone knew and knows right now. Someone maybe connected with the company."

"Wells Fargo?"

Clint nodded.

"You think Cratcher knew something?"

"I wouldn't be thrown by such a notion."

"But what about that business with the ears?"

"I think we both figure that might be—maybe is—a blind trail."

The lawman reached for the coffee pot, but Clint Adams held back his mug.

"What's the matter? You don't like my coffee? First you complain about my cigars. Now my coffee."

Clint cut his eye fast at the marshal, picking up right away on his droll way with humor. "No, I think your coffee's great, and surely as good tasting as one of those cigars."

Warshower chuckled at that.

"Fact," Clint continued. "I do believe you could sell that liquid to Clinch Fiddle."

"Like to preserve his corpses? Golly, that's a great idea!"

And they both had a good laugh at that.

It was dark when Clint left the marshal. The stars were thick in the sky. He looked up at the milky way, wondering how he was going to get a hold on this thing he'd somehow gotten into. There were so many elements, and not much sense to any of them. The most ridiculous was the story Ace DeWitt had tried to feed him. It was so obviously false. It was so damned fake that he had to see that the gambler had wanted him to see it as such. DeWitt wanted him to see his story that way. Which had to mean then that he wanted the Gunsmith to bite at something else; something that he didn't want to wrap up and hand as a package; something not laid out in detail. But there.

He had walked down the street and was standing outside the Moosehead, and now on an impulse he entered. The room was crowded, as it always was at that time of night. Indeed, for most of the night it would be crowded, he knew. Well, he decided, he would have a drink and do a little thinking, and sorting out. He had the definite feeling that he had all the elements before him, and that all he needed was to see them in proper perspective.

He was just lifting his glass of beer when he heard the voice at his back.

"Greetings, Mr. Stranger. I'm glad to see you."

He turned, and was instantly delighted.

"I don't mind you forgetting me, for a day or two, but not for this long." And she was laughing at him, at his sudden and obvious concern over maybe having hurt her.

They found an unused table, by luck, and sat down. He had just about forgotten Hallie, and he was glad to renew the relationship.

"Aren't you busy tonight?" he asked.

"I'm busy every night," she said brightly. "Like right now I'm busy with you. Did you miss me?"

"I sure did."

"I'm yours!" And she made a swooning gesture that gave him a big laugh. She was a delight to be with. A young woman with an open, positive energy, a rare one.

"You've been busy, haven't you," she said, lowering her voice.

"Matter of fact, yes I've been busy."

"Look at me now, like we were just having fun. There is something I want to tell you."

Her face was dead serious, and it gave him a shock as he realized what she was saying. Then suddenly she burst into laughter, pretending her role of the evening.

"Is somebody listening, watching?" Clint asked.

"I'm not sure, but I take it as a good rule to figure somebody is always listening when you don't want your business known."

"I sure agree with that," Clint said, leaning his forearms on the table, and hunching forward in the manner of intimate talk that would lead to the rooms upstairs.

"What do you want to tell me?" he said. "Can we go upstairs?"

"I was hoping you'd ask me. And don't worry!" She held up her hand to stop any objection on his part. "I know you don't pay for it. So I don't expect it!" At which point she made a face at him and thumbed her nose, reminding him of Melanie sticking her tongue out at him. But he didn't dwell on the comparison. He was already eager for bed. And as they crossed the crowded room heading for the stairs, he felt his erection driving against his trouser leg.

Clint Adams couldn't have wished for more, or better, he told himself as he lifted himself off the girl and lay down beside her. Both were perspiring, both had exercised themselves to the utmost, and even beyond. For Clint, it was one of his best times. Melanie had certainly been exciting, thrilling, and knew her tricks, but with this girl there was something many didn't have. She was—once you got through the armor—undeniably soft. Clint Adams sighed. He felt thoroughly grateful to his companion.

He lay still now, waiting for her to speak. He'd thought she might have spoken before they got into bed, with her "news," but she hadn't. First things first, obviously. But he could feel her beside him now working up to speaking.

"I want to tell you something," she said. "Maybe it isn't important, but you can decide that."

"Go ahead."

"There's . . ." And she hesitated, and getting up swiftly, went to the door on tiptoe and quickly unlocked and opened it.

"Thought somebody was outside."

"Is it that important?" he asked as she relocked the door.

"It's important enough to scare me."

"Tell me what it is."

"It's—well, it's nothing that really happened . . . "

She was sitting on the edge of the bed in her lovely nakedness, looking at the wall of her tiny room.

Clint Adams waited.

"It's not anything that happened, but it's someone . . ."

He studied the side of her face, trying to read her. "You're frightened," he said.

She nodded, and turned to face him, her bare breast brushing his bare arm. "I am. It's this man."

"One of your customers."

She nodded.

"What is he? What's he done?"

"He hasn't done anything."

But you don't want him to come see you? Is that it?"

"Something like that. I don't have to see him, I suppose. Or—no, I do. If I want to work here I have to see him."

"He owns the place? Something like that?"

"He owns the Moosehead and also the Hard Dollar, and just about everything else."

"I thought DeWitt owned the Hard Dollar."

"DeWitt's his partner. Sin Shavely owns everything, or so it seems."

"Sin Shavely. I don't know the name."

She shrugged. "Most people don't know him. I

only know him by accident. But he is the big man around here, and I understand, in the territory. At least everybody seems to be damned scared of him."

"But why are you scared of him?" Clint asked, watching the side of her face.

"I dunno. Something about him. Ugh! It's not even that he's so ugly. There's just something about him that . . . hell, that ain't human!" She stopped, sucking in her breath, and rubbing the palm of her hand over her stomach. "It gets me all tight in my belly, thinking of that slime!"

"So why are you telling me?"

"Look, I don't know your business. But I get around and I can't help hearing things. And . . . and I get it that you're looking for somebody. Something like that. What the hell, people know how you cut those two men trying to back shoot you. So people don't figure you're in Prairie Falls to teach Sunday school."

"You're warning me on this man Shavely. I appreciate it."

"You're welcome." And she was smiling at him again.

"Then how about my showing my appreciation to you."

"Anytime, sir. Any place." She leaned toward him, then stopped. "Only one thing. One very important thing. I like you, but don't get yourself a swelled head on it. But I want you to be careful."

"I'm always careful, young lady."

"Shavely is no ordinary person. He is the kind will do anything to get what he's after. Anything!"

"I've caught your drift. And I promise to be

careful. I think I understand the kind of man you're talking about."

She was smiling at him.

"I don't know if I picked the right time to tell you all that," she said.

"When would be better? What do you mean?"

She dropped her eyes for a moment, regarding his penis which was beginning to stir.

"I wanted to tell you before we made love."

"Then why didn't you?"

"Because some things can't be told when a man's got a hard on. Things like that, I mean. On the other hand, sometimes it's best to tell something when a man's horny. Depends."

He grinned at her. "What you're saying, miss, is that the only time a man has got any sense in him is right after he's had it."

"Right you are," she said, lying down and opening her arms and legs for him.

"Well, you can consider me without a drop of sense right now. Fact, I'm crazy as hell to mount you."

Her arms slid around his neck, then her hands ran softly down his back to find his buttocks. She ran a finger just in the crack, finally reaching way down to grab his balls from the rear.

"I want it so bad," she whispered. "I want you, I want you, all of you."

"You've got me," he said softly, as he began stroking his rigid penis into her.

Now they came together as one, dancing together, without a word, though each one's breath coming faster. She had her legs high up on him, and now she dropped them so that she could brace herself with them on the bed, as he rode her to their second climax.

When they finally disentangled themselves she said, "You're the best ever, my friend."

"You're not bad yourself."

Her laughter tinkled into his chest. "Mister, if you keep up that kind of lovemaking, it'll be me wanting to pay you."

But she realized then that her joke had gone sour, and she said, "I was only trying to be funny. Sorry."

"You were trying to be funny, so don't be sorry," he said quietly, lifting himself so he could look right into her face. "You were trying to be close to me. So there's nothing to be sorry about."

Chapter Ten

Miriam Landusky would never have been able to relate to anyone what she was feeling at the particular moment that she saw her sister Melanie coming down the staircase at the Junction House. It was a moment unparalleled in her life, and she told herself later that such a moment could never happen to her again.

All she could think to herself was how beautiful Melanie looked, and how finally after so much tribulation she had at last found her. And in a flash she realized how all her difficulties had been of her own making. That nice man, Mr. Adams, had simply pointed out to her the value of just taking one step at a time, and acting from her feeling of the particular moment. Which she was doing.

And there Melanie was, coming down the wide staircase, and the next thing she knew they were in each other's arms, and laughing and crying and laughing and each trying to talk at the same time. Never—never had Miriam ever in her short life felt so happy, so relieved, so absolutely grateful, grateful for the way things had worked out. And she saw how all her worrying and anticipating something possibly going wrong had been her nit-picking. That fiendish

148

habit she had, that old maid's habit as Melanie had long ago called it.

Then they had talked and had coffee in the dining room, and gone for a walk, and then come back to the hotel and had dinner. And all the time Miriam was asking herself why she had been so fearful of approaching Melanie, why had she put it off. But she knew. She knew it was that Melanie was beautiful, Melanie was popular, had always been beautiful and popular with everyone. While she, Miriam, had been the proverbial wallflower. Except that now, meeting Mr. Adams and that kindly Mr. Glendenning, she was beginning to feel somewhat otherwise. But she didn't pursue those thoughts. They were there, and maybe they were there to explain something to her—her mother, she knew, would have said something like that if she was alive now to talk to her. For here was Melanie, and Melanie was so glad to see her. It was as though a whole new life was opening for her. And indeed, it really was. And when she returned to Mrs. Thorpe's rooming house she took off her clothes, slipped on her nightdress and climbed in between the sheets, hugging her pillow. She began to cry, telling herself that she was happier than she had ever been in her life.

And yet, there came a sudden moment when she realized that something had been nagging her, right from the start. Right from the moment when she saw Melanie coming towards her. And she had shoved it away. But it wouldn't go away. It wasn't a big thing really. It was all right. Only it was there. It was that Melanie looked—older. Although, Miriam knew that "older" wasn't really the right word.

• • •

Melanie, on the other hand, at the same time that her very young and very innocent sister was hugging her pillow, was hugging Big Bob Glendenning's loins.

Later, attending to their ritual of champagne, Melanie told him about her sister, and how wonderful their meeting had been.

At first, Glendenning had been fearful that the young sister had told his paramour about their meeting, about his urging her to secrecy, and that he would try to help her. But Melanie said nothing that would indicate the girl had spoken about him. Something in him wanted to keep that chapter unknown to Melanie, for secrecy played a big role in his nature. But prudency won. He knew she would sooner or later discover that they had met and in a sense "plotted," and certainly under those circumstances what could be better than a clean sweep.

"But why didn't you tell me, Bob?"

"I was going to, my dear, but remember the meeting only happened yesterday, or maybe the day before. I can't remember. I was going to sound you out, you see, because I didn't know if she was really your sister. She could have been pretending, someone whom you didn't want to meet, or someone you didn't even know. Forgive me if I've done the wrong thing."

She giggled at him then, snuggling closer. "I think you're very noble. And I appreciate your noble instinct."

"Thank you, my dear." And he got up to refill their glasses.

When they had sipped more of that fine wine, he slipped his arm around her bare shoulders and moved down closer to her.

"Is something the matter?" he asked, feeling a change coming between them.

"Not really. I was just wondering why you did wait so long to tell me you'd met Miriam and talked with her."

"But, my dear, I told you as soon as I could." He dropped a confiding chuckle into her ear, his hand dropping to her bush. "After all, just as you recently told me yourself, I too believe in the practice of discussing events at only the appropriate time."

She opened her legs then, turning toward him. "I take it that now is not the time for discussion."

"Precisely, my dear. Precisely."

"Very well then, Cratcher is taken care of." The short man with the goatee—black, flecked with a wisp of gray—sat back in his chair and looked at his partner Harry "Ace" DeWitt.

They were seated in one of the private back rooms at the Hard Dollar. Drinks were in evidence, and certain papers that DeWitt had brought for Sin Shavely's perusal. Both men were smoking cigars, and the room was laced with streaks of blue gray smoke.

Sin Shavely, short, powerful, with very strong-looking hands, and cold eyes, let his eyes wander towards the ceiling.

"I'm glad to hear that things are moving well, Harry. We are . . . reaching towards the climax of our little adventure, and we want to be sure that there will be no mistakes."

"I couldn't agree with you more, Sin."

"I must admit that for a second or two I felt a slight concern when I heard that Cratcher's ears had been removed from the rest of him, fearing that such gratuitous brutality would call too much attention to the event. But then I of course realized you were tying it in with the revenge motive from the Kodl situation, where Cratcher had cut off Kodl's thumbs, and in consequence had angered some of Kodl's partisans."

"Quite," Ace DeWitt clipped the word with even more of the British than usual.

A silence fell.

After a moment Shavely spoke. He spoke slowly, his dark eyes gleaming out of his pale face as he focused right on the man seated across from him.

"I have allowed the silence to fall, Harry, so that you could tell me I was wrong. But you haven't. I don't like it when you lie to me, Harry."

A laugh broke from DeWitt's suddenly tight lips. "Not a lie, Sin. Simply a slight omission. Yes, you are astute as always, and you spotted the mistake that was made."

"I've told you before, Harry, that you don't need to cover up with me. We are partners. At least, I should add, at least at this level. And as such I expect openness. Now . . . now that's enough. My point is made. Let's get on with it."

"Of course, Sin. Of course." But DeWitt couldn't avoid it; Shavely had caught him. Well, drop it. The partnership was working well on all counts. Only that little slip . . .

"Although I would like to know who perpetrated that deed. Just let me know the name before we go on to the next subject."

"It was left to a man named Tiny Blue."

Shavely had taken an envelope out of his pocket and reached for the pen on the table which was between them. "Interesting name," he said, writing. He tossed down the pen and put the envelope into his pocket.

Shavely studied the ash on the end of his cigar. Then he put the cigar in his mouth and drew on it, emitting smoke towards the ceiling.

"I want to know more about this man who is called the Gunsmith."

Harry "Ace" DeWitt leaned onto the baize table-top, and smiled confidingly at his partner. "You were right, Sin. Adams is working for Wells Fargo. I got that straight from the mouth of the horse."

"Our noble friend, eh?"

DeWitt chuckled. "And I've fed Adams that story you told me, and as we both expected he didn't believe a word of it."

"But he suspects there's something else behind it." Shavely sat forward abruptly, as though playing an ace at the crucial moment.

DeWitt nodded, drawing on his cigar, while keeping his eyes on the other man. "He suspects, knows, there's something going on. Like we both said—and again I must remind you, Sin, that we *both* developed this maneuver—he knows that it was all snake oil, and he also knew that I knew he knew it."

Shavely said nothing. His eyes glittered at DeWitt for a moment, then he turned them towards the ceiling, as though looking up there for his thoughts, or for the exact words he wished to speak.

"Just to be absolutely clear, Harry." And with his head still raised towards the ceiling of the room he dropped his eyes down onto DeWitt, looking at him down the length of his nose.

"Glendenning has been doing as told." DeWitt's words came quickly. "His stage line has been taking one hell of a beating."

"Yes, I have heard very favorable reports on the collapse of the western stages. Pity, eh? So colorful, so romantic, and all that. But now we have the era of the Great Trains. And the towns that will spring up like mushrooms—all over the place. As you know, I have been in close contact with our man in Cheyenne."

DeWitt grinned. "Our, uh, territorial representative."

"Our private territorial representative," Shavely added.

"Sin, one question."

Shavely's eyebrows lifted as he lowered his head to look directly at his partner. "You want to know how Mr. X is."

"I do."

"He is following instructions, and more cannot be expected. Now then . . ." He cleared his throat suddenly, and sat up straight in his chair, with his elbows on the table. "Now then, we want a big hit, and I have arranged for our . . . regulators, if that's the right word, to handle it with their customary professionalism. We're getting close to the climax of our operation. Washington has agreed to certain things, and we can very shortly wind everything up. There'll be one or two important cleanup details of course."

Ace knew he shouldn't say it; he knew that flattering his partner was a sword with two points. As a gambler he understood full well how a man of Shavely's caliber loved flattery, but he also knew how that very same flattery built arrogance and contempt—in this case, towards himself. But he was a gambler, and a gambler—one who is worth the name—goes for the chips and leaves his own personal vanity outside the gambling hall. Hell, he had spent this good long while fanning Shavely's mountainous opinion of himself—even at his own loss in self-portraiture—and it had paid off. And he knew it would pay off now. All he had to do was put up with the little son of a bitch's arrogance.

"Sin," he said, smooth as a well-triggered holdout, "that was real clever of you getting Rhodes. I must say I admire that move."

Sin Shavely's little bullet eyes were close on DeWitt. "I hear that man can handle a rifle like most men do a six-shooter," he said. "It's obvious he's what we need." And as he drew on his cigar he was thinking how that smooth son of a bitch DeWitt just couldn't get over second dealing, no matter what was going on.

This time it was to be another train. For a more accessible or field headquarters, Miller established a camp in a wild canyon on Goose Creek, not far from their permanent camp in Wild Horse Canyon, but useful also as a decoy. Moreover, they would have the advantage of an alternate hideout. The Goose Creek camp offered fresh water, wood to burn, a mobile defensive position in the event of siege, and what was more, a remote location. For their first step—reconnaissance—a veteran who had ridden a number of times with Miller Rhodes in "the old days" was chosen as scout. Posing as a passing traveler the gentleman, one of whose names was Ike McGinnis, visited all the sparsely inhabited points along the rail route, looking for the most suitable locale for a holdup.

Traveling from town to town along the railroad, McGinnis found the ideal spot near Gantley. A short distance outside this hamlet the railroad tracks rose sharply as they approached a place called Double Buttes. Carefully, he surveyed the terrain before returning to Goose Creek, where Miller and the others awaited him.

It was a clear, cool night of early autumn when the express moved slowly into Gantley. A thin moon hung in the velvet sky as the train took on new cargo. The stubby locomotive threw sparks into the chilly air while it took on steam to leave Gantley behind. As it lurched into a smoother movement, a dark-clad, silent figure mounted the front end of the express car.

The train gathered speed for the mounting grade at Double Buttes as the dark figure leapt down into the engineer's cab.

"Stop the train!" he snapped.

The engineer, a burly man named Oxfoot, stared into the dark, chiseled face of Miller Rhodes.

As the train pulled down to a stop, three men appeared outside the cab. Oxfoot followed the orders to come down from the cab and go with the men to the express car.

"Tell your friend in there to open up," Miller Rhodes said, and there was menace in his words.

Oxfoot shouted out to the man inside the express car. In another moment the big, heavy door rolled open. Not a moment was lost in climbing up into the car.

Meanwhile, two of the gang forced the engineer to detach the heavily laden express form the rest of the train, and now the big work began.

As Miller ordered the express car guard to open the squat black safe, which was in a corner of the express car, a dim light twinkled ahead in a passenger coach. It was the train conductor. The light grew as the man approached to see what the trouble was.

"Go back and put out that light 'fore I shoot it out," shouted Rhodes. Without a moment's hesitation the conductor obeyed.

The express car man, meanwhile hovering in fright near the safe, risked his life by offering the information that he didn't have the combination. But Miller had matters in hand. He pointed to a giant side of beef that was in the car. "Get that, and get me the stuff . . ."

From outside the car one of the gang tossed in a black bundle of dynamite sticks to Miller's waiting hands.

Two men lugged the side of beef to the top of the safe, placed the dynamite underneath, and lit the fuse. Then, dragging the car man with them, they jumped from the car and ran to safety.

The explosion flared into the night, while the sides

of the express car bulged outward in a splintering crash.

As the outlaws climbed back into the car, the contents of the smashed safe lay scattered on the floor in front of them. The acrid fumes of dynamite lingered hazily in the air as they crammed the valuables into their open bags.

Less than half an hour from the time of the robbery the outlaws were pounding away towards their hideout at Goose Creek.

Later, when the celebrating had quieted some, Miller lay next to the Kid.

"It is real good to have you back, Miller."

He didn't make any reply for a moment, and she wondered why not, though she knew he could be moody at times.

Then finally he said, "Good to be back. Yeah, except you got it backwards, Kid. It's not good to have me back. I ain't bin away. But it's good to have you back, Kid."

Sin Shavely had just finished his breakfast in Meg Fiddle's Café when Ace DeWitt brought him the news of the successful holdup.

Meg saw them through a slit in the kitchen door as they conversed in whispers. They were the only customers in the place.

"Glendenning is ready to dump his stageline, by the way," DeWitt was saying. "And the B & R has got to be hurting, especially after last night."

To DeWitt's astonishment he saw Shavely's eyes light up. "Excellent. I see that we're ready to move. I didn't really go into this when we last met, but the land deal is closed, and we've cornered the whole of . . ." He opened his hands, nodding his head. "The whole of a mighty nice chunk of territory. It runs from Junction all the way up to Montana, and almost that same distance east and west."

"But what's the value of that, if I may ask?" DeWitt said, throwing a cautious eye at the kitchen door, and keeping his voice almost inaudible, even to his companion.

Shavely's face broadened in a gleaming grin. "I'll bet you think it's gold. You see, the railroad won't lay track over that area now. Nor will there be a stage route, unless we allow it. They're going to back off and go around by Gebo."

"The railroad."

"I am not talking about harvesting, friend."

"How soon?" DeWitt couldn't keep himself from feeling excited, even though his training as a gambler had taught the need to remain calm under all situations.

Shavely didn't answer him.

"But what are we talking about?" DeWitt asked again. "You say not gold. What then?"

"Water."

"Water! But my God, we went through all that, laying it on about the water pump to spur irrigation, and all that. You're not talking about that fake, for God sake!" In his excitement he had raised his voice, and Shavely shushed him as Meg Fiddle came in.

"You gents want anything? More coffee?"

"Nothing. We'd like to talk business a bit." Shavely reached into his pocket and handed her a twenty-dollar gold piece. "Just for a few minutes privacy."

Flushing, gripping the coin, Meg retreated into the kitchen closing the door behind her.

"She'll be all over town about that gold piece," DeWitt warned severely.

"That's what I want. I want the town to know that we're up to something. Something big. Something absolutely honest. Except it is something I don't want to appear as *selling*. You understand? I want them to come and demand to buy the land. Which they will do. Do you know why?"

"Why?" DeWitt asked, and his mouth hung open in spite of himself.

"Water." Sin Shavely said the word softly, with a liquid sound, as though he was pouring it. "Water," he repeated.

"I don't understand, Sin. We went through all that snake oil business about irrigation. I just said it a moment ago. I . . . I . . . "

"Water," Shavely said again. He beckoned with his finger for DeWitt to lean closer. "There is underneath that large section of land that I just a moment ago indicated to you, an almost equally large artesian lake."

"My God!"

"Ajax-Hiller and company has just acquired provisional title. You understand. The Billings & Rockland, and also the stage lines, that is to say, public transportation has first crack. But since they are finding this part of the country to be so unsafe, and therefore unprofitable for their enterprises, they are on the point of withdrawing and leaving the field to us. Since the government—and I have it on the very closest and most trustworthy authority—will sell this almost useless land to us, that is, to Ajax-Hiller. Me."

"Holy Mother of God!"

"I am pleased to see you so impressed, Harry."

"Those lots will be worth plenty!"

"You can see why I have remained silent on this aspect of our business activities. But I do expect you to continue to support the enterprise. Junction, of course, will become a boom town. Even more than it has been with the proximity of gold."

"I must say I am mightily impressed, Sin."

"You should be."

"And this is in the immediate offing."

"It is happening right now. I have people who keep me informed. Railroad people, and Glendenning who is unwittingly with us. And of course, our friend at Wells Fargo who has been so helpful with schedules and other details of shipments. Moreover, our men, your men I should say, since that is more in your department, are loyal and should be in view of the amounts of money they've been handling."

At that point the door of the café opened and two of the townspeople walked in for breakfast.

"Meg!" DeWitt called. "You've got customers."

"Let's take a walk," Shavely said. And when they were out in the street, taking DeWitt's arm for an instant's confidence, he said, "There is only one possible fly in the ointment."

"Adams," DeWitt said. "You're thinking of Adams."

"That man they call the Gunsmith, who's been

snooping around for Wells Fargo. I saw him in the land office at Billings."

"That's Adams."

"He must be taken care of."

"That can be arranged."

"Right away, Harry. We want no slips at this stage of things."

"I'm thinking of Tiny Blue."

"The one who took care of Cratcher?"

"That's the one. He isn't afraid of the Devil himself."

"I want you to have backup men, Harry. I mean . . . there must be no slips. I understand that man is very dangerous with a gun. And his snooping in the land office is not a good sign."

"He won't be able to beat a whole gang, Sin."

"That's more like it, Harry. That's much more like it. You work it out with whoever it is that's necessary. I want the best men. The top men. And today, Harry. Or, let's say no later than tomorrow."

The sun was just over the tops of the buildings now, forecasting a clear, warm day. The cool of the autumn night had vanished. And the town, stirring more now, knew that there was the seed of winter in the air. Harry DeWitt could feel it in his legs and back and the seat of his pants as he hurried along the street to get to the Hard Dollar. For an instant he wondered why Shavely had given him all that in the coffee shop, with the risk of people coming in, with the possibility of Meg Fiddle catching a key word here or there. He was something that Shavely. One smart bugger. And sure of himself. He had to be sure of himself to talk over such a big deal so casually, in such a place and at such a time. God, he hadn't even had his morning eye-opener yet. Well, all to the good. He had something to work on. And the cake that Shavely was cooking was going to be a rich one.

By the time he reached the Hard Dollar and was holding his morning glass in his hand, he had decided that the best way to handle the Gunsmith was with an "accident."

Chapter Eleven

News of the train holdup outside Gantley reached the Gunsmith almost as quickly as it did the authorities, thanks to Honus Warshower.

"I got need of a deputy, Adams," was how the marshal had put it.

Clint felt no objection to the request, and in fact realized it might help him get closer to what he was after. His main objective was still to find out who was the leak at Wells Fargo. Once again the bandits had known of a big shipment. It was clear that somebody was tipping them off.

Clint and Warshower talked with the train crew, plus some of the passengers who were still available.

"Interesting that this time the holdup men made no effort to disguise themselves," Warshower observed.

"I take that to mean they'll be pulling out. Maybe heading for greener grass," Clint said.

One of the passengers had spoken of Carisa, coming through the train with her hat, collecting wallets and other valuables.

Yet, it was the presence of Miller Rhodes that shook a number of people. The bandit was legendary, and a lot of people had even thought he was dead.

"It's obvious that Miller likes to be in the news and gossip," Clint said to Warshower when they were back in Prairie Falls. "Why else show himself so boldly."

"Well, like you say, it 'pears they'll be lighting out for new country."

"I think it means more than that," Clint said.

"How so?"

"They give me the feeling that they've completed something more than just some stage and train robberies. I've got the definite notion that there's a much bigger plan behind this whole picture than we're seeing."

"Like what?" the lawman asked, perking up his ears.

"I dunno. I spent some time in the land office this past couple of days."

"The land office?"

"In Billings."

"What'd you find there? More gold?" He chuckled at the thought.

"I found out that a man named Hiller, associated with an outfit called the Hiller-Ajax, or Ajax-Hiller company—the papers had it both ways—has been buying up land all around Junction and on up to the Montana line. But there's obviously no gold there. There's also not much in the way of water."

"Dry as a picked bone, that country," Warshower said. "I wouldn't want it."

Clint reached to his pocket for a quirly and lit it, striking the match on the cold stove in the center of the marshal's office. "You know a man named Shavely?"

"Sinwell Shavely, known as Sin Shavely. Everybody knows him, and nobody knows him. He's DeWitt's blind partner at the Hard Dollar. He's got gold instead of blood in his arteries and veins."

"Blind? You mean he's a kind of silent partner, keeps out of the way."

"He's one of the toughest, coldest, meanest, and just creepiest varmints a man would ever want to come across. That tell you enough?"

"Thanks. I didn't know he was a friend of yours."

"Very funny! And why are you asking about Sin Shavely?"

"He was around the office. Leaving when I got there, and he came back just when I was finished, and he didn't look too happy to see me."

"What you figger that old snake was up to?" The marshal leaned forward with his elbows on his knees and looked directly at the Gunsmith.

"That is just what I am wondering," Clint said. "But I know one thing."

"What is that?"

"I know he's been wondering what I was up to."

When the Gunsmith got back to the Junction House he found that he had a visitor.

"Don't worry," the guardian at the desk said to him, "it ain't anything purty. Fact, it is just a man." She grinned lecherously at him. "Disappointed you, huh?"

"I'm going to miss you when I'm gone, Carmela."

"Really!" She batted her long eyelashes at him, touched the edges of her astounding orange hair with her heavily ringed fingers, swayed a little. "I'll remember you said that, cowboy!"

Smiling, Clint made his way to the dining room to discover that his visitor was Cash Wilfong.

"Boy, you are a surprise!"

They shook hands warmly, while Clint noted a grayness had taken over his friend's face.

"Say, I wish I'd known you were coming. We could have looked over the robbery together. They blew up the whole express car."

"Sorry I missed it." Wilfong looked even grayer than at first, Clint thought. And when the Wells Fargo man said, "Look, can we get a drink here?" Clint knew something was off.

"Sure. Let's take over that table there." And he led the way to a table in the far corner of the room, which save for the sole waitress was deserted.

Watching his friend now, Clint felt a concern mounting.

"What have you got, Cash? It doesn't look good to me, judging by the way you're looking."

"It isn't good, Clint." He seemed to hesitate, then he straightened up, squared his shoulders and said, "I know you've been wondering who the leak has been at Wells Fargo."

Clint felt something sink inside him, but he didn't look away, he kept his eyes on Wilfong. Cash wouldn't meet his eyes now, he was looking down. But then, again, just as he'd done a moment before, he straightened and looked directly at the Gunsmith.

"I guess I do know who it is, Cash."

Wilfong nodded.

"Want to tell me why?"

"I have no excuse. Money."

"Of course money. But . . ."

Wilfong looked down at the drink he was holding in his hand, then lifted his eyes to face Clint. "Sick brother, wife not well either for that matter. I got into debt." He stopped.

"Do you want to tell me who's in on it. It isn't just the road agents, I know that."

"I can tell you what I know, Clint," Wilfong said, his face working. "But I only know the man who approached me. There's someone, something big in back of the whole thing, only I don't know who or what. Look, Clint, I'm giving myself up. When I came in on it I made them agree that no one was to get hurt. You will have noticed that for a while that agreement was carried out. But now . . . now things are different. I am getting out. I just have one request to ask you, one favor, Clint."

"Ask."

"I want to tell the company. Will you hold back talking to anyone? I wanted to tell you first, because I have not been straight with you."

Clint felt as though he was watching a man die. And yet, at the same time there was something else going on with Cash Wilfong. There was something there, something, yes, something he'd not seen before. A kind of substance, a grit, something that he liked. He knew what it was, but he didn't know any name for it.

"Cash, I am not saying anything to anyone. I sure hope you don't think I'd be turning my friend in."

In that moment Wilfong dropped his eyes, but then he looked up. His eyes were shining. "By God, you are a real friend, Clint." He lifted his glass of whiskey in a toast.

After taking a good swig he said, "That's just a part of what I have to tell you, my friend."

"There's more?" Clint said with an easy smile.

"Clint . . ." Cash Wilfong's voice was grave. "Watch your back trail, man."

"That bad, huh?"

"I don't know who it is running the big show, but I have got this feeling, a cold chill up and down my back. You know what I mean."

"I have been expecting it, and you're verifying it, which is helpful. Your warning helps sharpen me, Cash. I appreciate that."

"I wouldn't, I couldn't have done or said anything else," Wilfong said earnestly.

"I know that. And I am wondering, though not asking, whether it was that that brought you to tell me about yourself."

Cash Wilfong looked away.

"Let's not cut it too fine, Clint. Long as we're friends."

"Sure. I just wanted you to know that I know what you're doing for a friend." He stood up immediately after he said those words. "I think it'll be soon."

"Clint, the man who set me up in it was Glendenning."

"Wrecking his own stage line. Well, in a strange way that fits."

"I have heard that Big Bob has left the country. That's why I figure something's coming to a head. And why I tell you again to watch your back trail."

"That's what I am doing, my friend." And he started towards the door of the dining room.

"Count on me, Clint."

"I already am."

That night the Gunsmith slept away from his room at the Junction House. He knew that whatever way they were going to make their play it would be soon. Tomorrow at the latest, but it could be in the night. And more than likely they'd go for his back, On the other hand, they might try for an "accident." That would go down more with the population of Prairie Falls and Junction.

Then, how would they do that? How would he do it, if he was handling such an event?

He had come down to the livery barn and made himself a hay bed in Clint Fiddle's Hayloft Inn that the old boy had told him about the first day he had hit town. Fiddle hadn't been about and so he'd just walked in and helped himself to bedding and space. It was a good spot to be in. He was near the edge of town, and Duke was at hand. He could hear the big black horse nickering below in his stall, wanting him to climb down and give him a can of oats no doubt.

He spent some time going through all the possibilities that might be used in the effort to kill him. But then he grew tired, and closed his eyes.

He slept as he slept on the trail—half awake. And in the predawn he opened his eyes and sat up. It would be today. He knew this.

When he climbed down from the loft Clint Fiddle, the hostler, was there.

"Mornin'." He was chewing fast on a fresh plug.

"Anybody about?" Clint asked after throwing water on his face from one of the horse buckets.

"You expectin' company?" The hostler squinted at him. He had been forking hay, and now he leaned on his pitchfork, and blew his nose one handed between his fingers, narrowly missing his own feet.

"I dunno. I'd appreciate anything you can tell me like someone maybe hasn't been invited to the party."

"I read you."

The old man said no more, but started forking more hay to the horses in the stalls.

A few moments passed while Clint decided he needed some coffee.

As he started out of the livery Clint Fiddle said, "See some of the Wild Horse and Crossbones' boys rid into town. Likely a mite thirsty, workin' hard like they do."

Clint stopped just inside the door of the big barn and surveyed the street. He was thinking of the Fiddle brothers, each of whose name started with C. Then he saw the cat slipping in around the door jamb.

"Somebody out there, I do believe," Clint Fiddle said, his voice low as he stopped forking hay.

"I believe he just walked by. That your cat, Mr. Fiddle?"

"It is."

"Cat got a name?"

"Yup."

"Don't tell me. Is it Clarke? Clementine? Clarice?"

"Wrong. The name is Cain." And Clint Adams was glad to see that the old man didn't crack a smile or a wink as he said that.

* * *

He had started slowly up the street watching the rooftops, the alleys, making sure that the newly risen sun didn't hit his eyes. He felt good, loose, alert, and as balanced as any of the hair triggers he'd put into the guns he'd repaired.

Warshower was in his office, checking out a couple of shotguns and a Winchester rifle. He had ammunition stacked on the table.

"Somebody told me today's the Fourth of July," he said.

"It's as good a time as any for the Fourth," Clint said.

"See you're still in town."

"Where did you expect me to be, Marshal?"

"Still in town."

They were silent a moment, then the marshal nodded towards the table with the weapons and ammo loading it down. "Help yourself. It don't hurt to have extra to my mind."

"Thanks." But he made no move towards the table.

"Company's expected anytime now," Warshower said.

"Why don't you stay out of it, Marshal. It isn't your fight."

"It ain't yours either, Adams. It's this town's fight. Exceptin' there ain't nobody fighting, or even thinking of fighting."

Clint had crossed to the window. "I wouldn't be so sure of that."

"What you see there?" Warshower looked up from his work of checking his weapons.

"I see an awful lot of Fiddles out there, and some others too. And it is fixing to rain."

"Fiddles?"

"Clancy. Clint, Clem, Clinch . . . and others like I said."

He had just stepped to the door when he heard the drumming hooves, and as he stepped into the street he could feel the reverberation coming through the ground.

"Jesus H. Christ! They're gonna stampede!" War-shower had come out fast and was standing beside him, holding a sawed-off shotgun.

"Stampede!" somebody shouted from an upstairs window. "My God, it's longhorns! Longhorns!"

Now the roar was closer. And again the street was bare of people, yet suddenly now filled with the yells of the oncoming riders who were driving the rear of the herd. The cattle leaders had broken into a faster run, the sound of their gait ominous as they gained momentum under the pistol shots of the riders behind them.

The Gunsmith leaned forward to get a good look. All at once he felt a drop of water on the back of his hand. Looking up he saw the sky was heavily overcast. In the next moment lightning forked the gray underbelly of the thick clouds, and a crack of thunder drove right through the town. The leaders of the herd broke wild-eyed down the street. The riders in the rear were encouraging them. The leaders of the herd were still clearing the boardwalks and some pillars that supported some of the canopies. But those behind were not so careful, and two, now three posts were struck and finally a canopy fell into the street.

"Get inside!" Clint shouted above the din. And he turned toward the office, shoving open the door. Warshower was right behind him.

In the next second he saw the men standing spread across the back wall. They'd come in from the back of the building. He had the Colt out and up, drilling one of them through the eye, another in the chest. He felt Warshower going down beside him, but not without the marshal winging the third man.

Two dead and one wounded. And Warshower. The marshal had been hit in the arm.

"I'm all right," he shouted as the herd of cattle roared by outside, crashing into the walls of the buildings next to the office, a longhorn knocking out one of the office windows.

"You dry-gulching son of a bitch!" roared the lawman at his prisoner. "I oughta blow yer balls off, you fucking hero!"

The gunman had thrown down his weapon and stood there, holding his wounded arm tenderly, his face grimacing with pain.

Suddenly now as the sound of the herd receded, a crash of gunfire slammed into the side and front of the building. Taking a fast look, the Gunsmith saw that there were sharpshooters on the roofs across the street, and men in two of the alleys.

Then suddenly the firing stopped.

Warshower spun on their prisoner, shoving a gun barrel right against his face. "You make a sound to let on we're here and you're dead."

The man was big, bigger than the marshal. He must have been feeling better with his wound for he started to open his mouth and Warshower slammed him right in the face with the gun barrel. "Next time you move or try to call out I'll kill you," he said to the prone gunman, who was out cold.

"Adams! Warshower!" A voice suddenly called from the street. "We know you're in there. Come on out with yer hands up and you won't be hurt."

"Go to hell," said the Gunsmith. Speaking to his wounded companion, "If he thinks we'd believe that, then he knows we'd believe anything."

"The bastards," snarled Warshower. "I think that was Rhodes."

As if to verify his statement a fresh voice now called out, "Rhodes! You yeller belly. Throw down your gun and I'll fight you fair!"

"God, that's Wilfong!" The words burst from Clint as he recognized the voice.

"You can see 'em both out this window," Warshower said.

Clint moved over, keeping away from the window, sure that someone had a sight on it. And then he saw Miller Rhodes standing on the boardwalk across the street.

"Come on out whoever you are," Rhodes called out, signaling the firing to stop.

"There he is," Warshower said. And Clint saw Cash Wilfong walking across the street. He must have been in an alley.

"Want me to shoot him, Miller?" someone called out.

"I'll have that pleasure," the bandit chief said. "Don't anybody even think of hurting a hair on his head. He is mine." He shouted out a laugh. "Hey, Gunsmith! Come on out and save your friend. I know you bin working for Wells Fargo, you lousy son of a bitch. Come on out and save your friend!"

"Don't go out there," said Warshower. "You'll be dead before you can shake hands with yourself."

Rhodes was shouting again. "Gunsmith, come on out and save yer pal. I want to show you and everybody here who is the fastest gun. On account of it sure ain't you, you lousy son of a bitch!" He spat, kicking the dirt at his feet.

"He's working himself up," Warshower said as he saw Clint start toward the door. "God, don't go out there. You and Wilfong'll both be cut down."

"I want you to back me. Come on."

"I'd be glad to, Adams, but I sure don't believe in suicide. Not at my age."

"You want some insurance?"

"You got any, fer Christ sake!"

"When you come out, Marshal, don't get in the line of your deputies' fire, but aim for that big bugger on the roof of the bank."

And before the astonished marshal could reply, Clint had opened the door of the office and stepped out, holding his hands out to show he was carrying only his holstered six-gun.

The entire town seemed to have been struck dumb. At least that was how Marshal Honus Warshower described it later when relating the incident. He had followed Clint out a few paces behind him, when he'd realized the full situation.

Clint Adams had walked partly across the street to face the bandit chief. His vision, however, took in more than Miller Rhodes. He saw the woman not very far away from Rhodes and several of his men. But he didn't see Tiny Blue. Not a good sign.

He had noted that the sky was clearing, and had also marked the fact that a number of men had left to corral the stampeded herd before they got too spread out. Miller, Clint realized, was skirting overconfidence. In a way he was surprised that the legendary bandit would be that foolish, but then he knew too that men like Rhodes basked in their own story, and eventually—if they lived that long—began to believe their own tales of heroism and derring-do. Well, all to the good. For he was going to need every ounce of assist. He saw Cash Wilfong standing very still only a few yards away, and mostly he saw Rhodes, smiling, at ease with himself and his big audience. But he still did not see Tiny Blue.

Taking an instant, he cut his eye quickly to the sky, noting that the clouds were clearing. The sun was at his back, though behind a cloud. Again all to the good if he could stall another moment or two. He looked at the big glass window right behind Rhodes, the storefront of the General Feed and Hardware Co.

And now they were facing each other. Miller Rhodes' face was filled with a laughing sneer.

"Always been hearing about you, Gunsmith. Over the years. Always hearing what a hotshot you are. Heerd tell you could shoot the asshole out of a rattlesnake standing on your head. Is that true, Gunsmith?"

"Must be if you believe it. Rhodes."

"I don't believe it, Gunsmith. I don't believe you're the fastest gun that ever walked God's good green earth! Do you, Gunsmith?"

Behind him, Clint felt the sun coming out from behind the cloud as the warmth touched his shoulders and back. In that same instant he saw in the window of the General Feed and Hardware Co. Tiny Blue sighting him from the top of the roof in back of him.

Miller Rhodes said something, but the Gunsmith didn't hear. Rhodes' big hand swept down. Tiny Blue was still sighting right into his back.

Later, Warshower and the other witnesses had half a dozen different versions, but there was only one that counted.

Smooth as water, the Gunsmith drew, as he dropped to the street, landing on his back and twisting, rolling, firing right at Tiny Blue who received the bullet in his throat. Even before the bandit's rifle hit the street below, Miller Rhodes had got his in the chest. He died still holding his unfired six-shooter.

Suddenly a shout went up from the onlookers. Clint Adams was still on the ground rolling. A shot rang out, and street dirt splattered into his face. And then another shot from a rifle cut into the tableau, and rising, the Gunsmith saw Carisa Bolero grabbing her arm which had been shattered by the bullet fired from Cash Wilfong's Winchester.

There was a moment of stunned silence, and then two of the Rhodes men went for their guns. In the instant a battery of rifles and handguns appeared in the hands of more than a dozen men, and a few women who had been watching from the boardwalks.

"Throw up yer hands, you buggers!" roared Clint Fiddle. "Anyone make a move he'll have the honor of being gut shot by one of us Fiddles, of which there is men and women more than enough to handle you bastards. I mean, right now!"

Clint was on his feet staring at the crowd of Fiddles, including Meg who was grinning firmly at him.

"You were right, Adams," Warshower said, coming up to him.

"Right?"

"You said I'd better keep out of line of my deputies' fire. Them boys there didn't think of that."

Later, as they handled their drinks in the quiet of the marshal's office, Clint filled Warshower in on the whole story of Sin Shavely and DeWitt and Glendenning, while Cash Wilfong sat in silence.

"I'll send a wire on them," Warshower said. "They won't get far. 'Course, proving up on 'em might be something else."

"That isn't my department," the Gunsmith said.

Warshower chuckled. "Nor mine." He looked over at Cash Wilfong who had been silent most of the time. "That was good shooting, and at the right time." He nodded first at Cash, then at Clint.

"You saved me there, Cash. I won't forget," Clint said simply.

"I got a question. Two questions, matter of fact," Warshower said.

"Shoot. I mean, let's hear it." Clint laughed at his little joke.

"What about the leak at the Wells Fargo office. Didn't you tell me you suspected something there?"

Clint stood up. It was time to go. "That I did. But sometimes one can't be sure."

"Was there somebody?"

"There was," Cash Wilfong said, standing up. "The . . ."

But Clint Adams cut him off. "The man turned himself in is what I heard. Sorry, Cash, I interrupted you."

There was a slow grin on Cash's face. "I was about to say the same thing."

With his hand on the door jamb, Clint turned back to the marshal of Prairie Falls and Junction. "You said you had two questions, Honus. What was the other?"

"How'd you know them Fiddles was out there acting as volunteer deputies! I mean, I wouldn't of gone anywhere near that outside if I hadn't of known they was backing us. But how'n hell did you know that? You couldn't see them!"

Clint half turned back to the man who had asked the question. "I didn't know it," he said. "I was just hoping they were."

And with a wink at Cash Wilfong he led the way out to the street.

Once again it was early dawn. He had saddled Duke and led him outside the livery. The big black gelding was feeling his oats, ready to go.

"Where to, boy?" Clint asked him. Receiving no answer, though not expecting one, he looked at the lightening sky.

"You be leaving, huh?"

He had heard the hostler coming up behind him. Without turning, he said, "Reckon."

"Watch yer back trail. You never know what kind of friends those buzzards got."

"I'll do it." He looked across the seat of his saddle

at Clint Fiddle, and grinned. Then he stepped into the stirrup and mounted. With a nod at the hostler he laid his reins across Duke's neck and the big horse started up the street.

"Heading north, huh?"

"I favor the Sweetwater country," Clint said.

There was no one about in the street, and it was why he liked the time for leaving a place. It was usual from him to pull out in the dawn time. He didn't especially like saying good-byes. He'd seen Miriam Landusky the evening before for a brief moment. He was pleased that things were working out for her with her sister. For a few moments it had crossed his mind to dally with the young lady, but somehow it wasn't the moment. Funny how you knew a thing like that. He was sorry Melanie wasn't around, but then later realized he was just as glad. It was definitely time to move on.

He was abreast of the Moosehead when suddenly a door at the side of the building opened and he saw the girl.

"You weren't going to say good-bye," she said. "I saw you from my window upstairs."

"I don't like good-byes," the Gunsmith said.

"Then come on in and say hello," the girl said.

And when they were upstairs and he was lying beside her in her bed, he said. "Hello, Hallie."

She smiled at him and ran her fingers along the side of his face.

The Gunsmith had been thinking of the Sweetwater. He felt so beautifully quiet after their lovemaking. But now, as Hallie's fingers moved down onto his chest, his belly and loins, he found what he had known all along—the Sweetwater would be there no matter when he got to it, and there was always still time to not say good-bye.

Made in the USA
Middletown, DE
27 December 2021

57112722R00111